I0763511

THE FOURTH REICH

The Fourth Reich

NOTE: This is a work of fiction. Names, characters, places, and incidents are the product of the author's imagination or are used fictitiously, and any resemblance to actual persons, living or dead, business establishments, events or locales is entirely coincidental.

ISBN: 978-1-7348524-7-9 (hardback)
978-1-7348524-9-3 (paperback)
978-1-7378736-0-0 (ebook)

Printed in the United States of America

THE FOURTH REICH

A Jeannie Loomis Novel

with Sean Delaney

GARY J. ROSE

OTHER BOOKS BY GARY J. ROSE:

JEANNIE LOOMIS NOVELS

Ark of the Covenant – Raid on the Church of Our Lady Mary of Zion

Star Chamber

Forgotten Plans

House of Special Purpose

Time Game

Thin Blue Line

NON-FICTION

Towards the Integration of Police Psychology Techniques to Combat Juvenile Delinquency in K-12 Classrooms

Hitting Rock Bottom (Amazon best-seller)

Teaching Inside the Walls

How to Create a Public-School Military-Style Book Camp Academy

To Mom, whom I lost several weeks after she proof-read this manuscript's rough draft. I know my biggest fan is in heaven with my dad, friends, and family.

Special thanks to Drs. Fred and Jane Vallier of Vallier Communications Consultants for another great job of editing.

"When you stop dreaming or using your imagination, you start to die."

—Gary J. Rose

A NOTE TO READERS

Hitler's Third Reich collapsed 76 years ago on April 30, 1945, the date of Hitler's suicide. However, at the time of this novel's publication, its successor--the Fourth Reich--is alive and well according to some European and US (United States) journalists, politicians, and activists' claims.

The term "Fourth Reich" has been used to reference a variety of movements. Neo-Nazis have used it to describe their envisioned revival of an ethnically pure state, mostly in reference to, but not limited to, Nazi Germany. Neo-Nazis envision the Fourth Reich as featuring Aryan supremacy, anti-Semitism, Lebensraum (the territory that a state or nation believes is needed for its natural development), aggressive militarism, and totalitarianism.

Today, the "Fourth Reich" is a concept synonymous with the resurgence of Nazism, but more ominous than "neo-Nazi": it suggests something concrete and actual rather than an aspirational, abstract idea. The Fourth Reich suggests that right-wing extremists are on the brink of power or have already attained it. Upon establishing the Fourth Reich, German neo-Nazis propose that Germany should acquire nuclear weapons and threaten to use them as a form of nuclear blackmail to reinstate Germany's pre-1937 boundaries.

The term, "Fourth Reich," was first used as a rallying cry in the 1930s by German Nazi regime opponents representing a broad political spectrum, from left-wing German exiles in Paris who produced a "Draft Constitution for a Fourth Reich" in 1936, to conservative monarchists who spoke of a future post-Nazi Fourth Reich of Christian unity.

Jewish refugees in New York who referred to their neighborhood as the "Fourth Reich" were equally strange bedfellows. Comprised of renegade Nazis belonging to Otto Strasser's schismatic "Black Front" organization, they envisioned the Fourth Reich as a place where "genuine" National Socialism would one day be realized (History Today Ltd. Company #1556332).

It is important in an educational environment that sometimes shuns the study of history to understand how the West has coped with a nightmare that never happened--the creation of a Fourth Reich. On the one hand, it reminds us that not long ago much of the world was paralyzed by concerns that proved to be groundless. On the other hand, what would happen if our fear of Nazis returning to power were grounded in a real threat: the resurrection of Adolf Hitler himself?

"Cloning" refers to the production of genetically identical copies of organisms. Copied material with the same genetic makeup as the original constitutes a clone. Researchers have cloned a wide range of biological materials including genes, cells, tissues and even an entire organism such as a sheep. Basically, to create a clone, scientists transfer the DNA from an animal's somatic cell into an egg cell that has had its nucleus and DNA removed. The egg develops into an embryo that contains the same genes as the cell donor, and that is subsequently implanted into an adult female's uterus to grow and develop.

In nature, some plants and single-celled organisms such as bacteria produce genetically identical off-springs through a process known as asexual reproduction. A new individual originates from a copy of a parent organism's single cell.

Natural clones, also known as identical twins, occur in humans and other mammals, and are produced when a fertilized egg splits, creating two or more embryos that carry almost identical DNA. Each identical twin has nearly the same genetic makeup as the other but is genetically different from either parent.

During the past 50 years, scientists have conducted cloning experiments using a wide range of animals and a variety of techniques. In 1979, researchers produced the first two genetically identical mice by splitting a mouse embryo and implanting each of the embryos into an adult female mouse's womb. Shortly thereafter, researchers produced genetically identical cows, sheep, and chickens by transferring the nucleus of a cell taken from an early embryo into an egg that had been emptied of its nucleus.

It was not until 1996, however, that researchers succeeded in cloning the first mammal from a mature (somatic) cell taken from an adult animal. After 276 attempts, Scottish researchers produced Dolly, a lamb that originated from the udder cell of a 6-year-old sheep. Two years later, researchers in Japan cloned eight calves from a single cow; however, only four survived.

In addition to cattle and sheep, other mammals cloned from somatic cells include cats, deer, dogs, horses, mules, oxen, rabbits, and rats. Not surprisingly, even a rhesus monkey has been cloned through embryo splitting.

But what about human cloning? Despite several highly publicized claims, human cloning still appears to be fiction. There currently is no solid scientific evidence that anyone has cloned human embryos.

In 1998, scientists in South Korea claimed to have successfully cloned a human embryo, but they said the experiment was interrupted very early when the clone was just a group of four cells. In 2002, Clonaid, part of a religious group that believes humans were created by extraterrestrials, held a news conference to announce the birth of what it claimed to be the first cloned human, a girl named Eve. However, despite repeated requests by the research community and news media, Clonaid has never provided any evidence to confirm the existence of this clone, nor the other 12 human clones it purportedly created; thus, it fell into the fake science category.

In 2004, a group led by Woo-Suk Hwang of Seoul National University in South Korea published a paper in the journal, Science, in which the group claimed to have created a cloned human embryo in a test tube. However, an independent scientific committee later found no proof to support the claim, and in January 2006, Science announced that Hwang's paper had been retracted.

From a technical perspective, cloning humans and other primates is more difficult than cloning other mammals. One reason is that two proteins essential to cell division known as spindle proteins are located very close to the chromosomes in primate eggs. Consequently, removal of the egg's nucleus to make room for the donor nucleus also removes spindle proteins, interfering with cell division.

In other mammals such as cats, rabbits and mice, the two spindle proteins are spread throughout the egg. Thus, removal of the egg's nucleus does not result in loss of spindle proteins. Moreover, some dyes and the ultraviolet light used to remove an egg nucleus can damage the primate cell and prevent it from growing.

The news that researchers have used cloning to make human embryos for the purpose of producing stem cells may have many wondering if it will ever be possible to clone a human. Although unethical, experts say it is biologically possible. But ethics aside, the sheer amount of resources needed to do it is a significant barrier.

For instance, animal cloning requires removal of the egg cell nucleus. The process also removes proteins essential for cell division. This is not a problem when cloning mice because the new mouse embryo can recreate these proteins, skill primates are not equipped to accomplish this. Researchers believe that may be one reason attempts to clone monkeys have failed.

Moreover, cloned animals often have genetic abnormalities that prevent embryo implantation in a uterus and cause the fetus to spontaneously abort or predispose the animal to die shortly after birth. These abnormalities are common because cloned embryos only have one parent, meaning that the molecular process known as "imprinting" does not occur properly in a cloned embryo, a process that selectively silences certain genes from one parent or the other.

Imprinting problems can also result in extremely large placentas, leading to fetal blood flow limitations. The extremely high death rate and the risk of developmental abnormalities associated with cloning renders human cloning unethical. Of course, that presumes that the medical professionals involved in the cloning process are ethical in their practice.

Josef Mengele, the Nazi SS doctor assigned to the Auschwitz death camp and who opportunistically conducted genetic research on thousands of human subjects would not have been bothered with this ethical question. His experiments focused primarily on twins with no regard for their health or safety, and earned him the nickname, "Angel of Death." Mengele used Auschwitz as an opportunity to continue his anthropological studies and research into heredity, using inmates as human subjects. He was particularly interested in identical twins and people with heterochromia iridum (eyes of two different colors).

The work of fiction herein, poses the possibility of a vast network of Nazi supporters yearning for the rise of the Fourth Reich--with a resurrection of its figure head, Adolf Hitler, brought about through cloning.

Background information: Although it has been established that Hitler died in his Berlin bunker, rumors of his escape abound. Research by both the Soviets and the United States proved that Hitler did not flee to Argentina in a submarine, nor did he hide in an Antarctica base.

In late April 1945 as Soviet forces stormed Berlin, Hitler made plans for his suicide by testing SS-supplied cyanide pills on his Alsatian dog, Blondi, and then dictating a final will and testament. Two days earlier, Mussolini had been shot by a firing squad and publicly hung by his feet in a suburban square in Milan, Italy. A similar fate seemed inevitable for Hitler.

Late on April 30, the bodies of Hitler and his new bride, Eva Braun, were found in the bunker with a bullet hole in Hitler's temple. Braun's corpse exhibited no visible external wounds, but the room distinctly smelled of almonds, a sign of cyanide poisoning. The bodies were carried upstairs and out through the bunker's emergency exit. In the bombed-out garden behind the Reich Chancellery, the soldiers wrapped their Führer in a Nazi flag, doused the bodies with gasoline and set them on fire.

The bodies burned throughout the afternoon as the Soviets occasionally shelled the area. Even though the bodies were not completely destroyed, the fire was eventually extinguished in the early evening and the remains were buried in a shallow shell crater.

On the morning of May 2, a private in the Soviet Army noticed an oblong patch of recently disturbed soil as he and the 79th Rifle Corps searched the Chancellery. He began to dig, thinking he might uncover some hastily buried Nazi treasure. Instead, his shovel hit bone and then legs. He called his commanding officer who ordered an exhumation. The soldiers dug up the bodies of two dogs (thought to be Blondi, Hitler's pet German Shepherd, and one of her pups) and the badly burned remains of two people. Following autopsies, Soviet soldiers moved what remained of Hitler's body to a different gravesite outside Berlin proper. This would be just one of several moves the corpse would make during the following few decades.

In early June of that same year, the Soviets reburied Hitler's remains in a forest near the town of Rathenau. Eight months later, they moved it again, this time to the Soviet Army garrison in Magdeburg. It remained there until March 1970 when the Soviets abandoned the garrison and turned it over to the East German civilian government. The remains came under the authority of the former Soviet secret police, the KGB, and finally, the FSB.

After months of negotiations, Russia's FSB secret service--with the blessing of Putin and the Russian state archives--gave researchers permission to examine the remains' skull fragments and bits of teeth. The skull section had a hole through its left side with black charring around the edges, a marking consistent with the effects of a bullet wound. Although scientists were not allowed to remove samples from the skull, they noted that its shape seemed "totally comparable" to radiographies of Hitler's skull taken a year before his death.

Gruesome photos of the teeth included in the study showed a jaw made mostly of metal. At his death, Hitler had only four remaining teeth. The few that survived were misshapen, brown at the base, and flecked with white tartar deposits.

The analysis corroborated frequently cited claims that Hitler was a vegetarian, but the observation could not conclusively prove whether he took cyanide before the gunshot wound occurred. Bluish deposits on his false teeth, the researchers wrote, suggested a variety of questions: did a chemical reaction take place between his fake teeth and the cyanide at the moment of his death, during his cremation, or while the remains were buried?

In the absence of analysis samples, it is impossible to know for sure. It is not known if he used an ampule of cyanide to kill himself or whether he was killed by a bullet to the head. It could have been both.

In April 2018, the English publication of a Russian interpreter's memoir revealed how she had been entrusted with a set of teeth in 1945 and tasked with cross-checking them against Hitler's dental records. They matched and have remained in Russian hands ever since.

OATH OF ALLEGIANCE TO ADOLF HITLER

"I swear by God this holy oath, that I will render to Adolf Hitler, Führer of the German Reich and People, Supreme Commander of the Armed Forces, unconditional obedience, and that I am ready, as a brave soldier, to risk my life at any time for this oath."

ONE

The yellow Cessna 208 Caravan seaplane circled the inlet twice before setting up for its final approach. The nearly 38-foot-long plane could be heard from the villa as it passed overhead. Upon hearing its approach, Dr. Wolfgang Hausser put down his cup of coffee, closed the manila folder on his desk, closed the lid of his laptop and glanced at his watch, noting the seaplane was arriving on time.

Outside his villa's front door awaited a black Jeep Gladiator and driver. A second man approached from Dr. Haussers' side carrying an AR-15 rifle. After Hausser climbed into the Jeep's front passenger seat, the armed guard climbed in behind.

The four-minute drive from the shore to the villa was stiflingly hot. The small unnamed tropical island off the coast of Argentina was unusually humid for this time of year, and the Jeep's air conditioning system did little to cool the armed guard seated in the rear. Since the doctor loved the fresh smell wafting in from the ocean, the windows were down--defeating the purpose of the air conditioner.

The six bedrooms/five bathrooms villa was constructed under Dr. Hausser's guidance and designed to accommodate 14 guests. Three bedrooms were spacious and intended for guests, the other three were of standard size and décor. Ironically, once the villa was completed, Hausser never had that many guests at one time. He preferred to be left alone with his work.

The master suite had a jetted whirlpool bath which Hausser used religiously to ease his osteoarthritis discomfort. Although he felt vulnerable lying in the tub, he was always much more comfortable after a daily 20-minute hot water soak. He received some relief basking in the sun beside the large swimming pool flanking the main residence, but it did not compare to the whirlpool's soothing effects.

Several large picture windows offered ocean inlet views from the spacious sunken living room furnished with hand crafted wooden furniture and imported woolen rugs. Heavy overhead timbers, hardwood floors and a stone fireplace completed the feeling of the mountain chalet that Hausser had lived in for most of his life in Austria. It was a room used only a few times in the winter. Sometimes he referred to it as his "Eagles Nest," referring to Adolf Hitler's mountaintop retreat near the town of Berchtesgaden in the Bavarian Alps.

A spacious dining area adjoined the living area and was punctuated with more large windows offering ocean views. It proved to be an excellent place to dine and entertain guests. A large professional kitchen with two sinks and modern appliances provided the kitchen help with conveniences they could never dream to enjoy in their own meager homes.

The game room with pool table and board games was rarely used, but someday after Hausser's leave of the villa, it would provide a convenient place for a family to relax at the end of a busy day. Of course, the "family" Hausser envisioned as future occupants would be higher-ups in the SS.

Every detail of the villa's design took advantage of its private ocean inlet setting. Large gardens surrounded the estate with several paths leading to a private ocean-front beach and docking area--and, of course, to the hospital. Jungle flora and fauna—especially Macaws and other birds--incessantly tried to reclaim their environment and had to be kept at bay.

As a local boy was securing the seaplane to the dock that extended about 50 feet into the cove, the side door of the Cessna opened and a thin blond-haired male wearing a blue baseball hat, white pants, and button-down shirt emerged. He removed his cap, wiped sweat from his brow, and then replaced it. Seeing Dr. Hausser approaching the dock, he waved.

"Herr Doctor, how are you?" he said, as his unsteady legs carried him along the dock.

"Fine. And you Major?"

"I cannot complain. No one will listen anyway. Is that not what everyone says?"

While pleasantries were shared; a second seaplane circled the cove. The pilot of the American Champion yelled at the errand boy to release the plane from the dock, and quickly taxied it out of the inlet. Once in the clear, he accelerated the engine, lifted the plane above the water and began to gain altitude as the other plane made its approach. A black Mercedes drove up and parked next to the Jeep Gladiator occupied by a lone driver. "Come, come. He will bring the others," Dr. Hausser said, pointing to the other vehicle.

Hausser's shirt was sticking to his chest and back by the time he and his first guests reached the villa. "Please, help yourself to refreshments while I change my shirt. I love the tropics, but the heat is sometimes unbearable," he said, climbing the stairs and heading toward his bedroom.

The major did not hesitate to pour himself a vodka soda over three ice cubes he slid inside. While removing his cap and rolled the icy glass across his forehead, he heard the Mercedes arrive, followed by four doors slamming shut. As he walked toward the front door, several individuals entered.

"Major," said an elderly short and stocky male with dark hair and wire-rimmed glasses. "It is so nice to see you."

"Yes Captain, and how was your flight?"

"Fine, fine. But you know what they say, it is not the flight that matters, it is the crash that spoils everything." Everyone nodded in agreement.

Dr. Hausser emerged from the upstairs and approached his guests. "Gentlemen, please help yourself to refreshments. Sophia, please bring in food for our guests." Sophia and another native girl quickly came from the kitchen, each carrying several plates of fruit and sea food. "Please, everyone. Fill a plate since there is much to be discussed."

Hausser poured himself a cup of mango juice, but no food. He walked around a large wooden desk located in front of three leather couches set in a U-shaped arrangement. While his guests ate, drank, and socialized, he removed a large binder and Mac laptop computer from a desk drawer. Removing a thumb drive from his pocket, he placed it into a USB port, then plugged a cable into a second port. Spinning his chair halfway around and using a remote control, he activated a mechanism that lowered a screen from the ceiling. Taking the descending screen as a cue that the briefing was about to start, the guests searched for a seat, balancing their plates and drinks until they found a landing site.

"Gentlemen, how rude of me," Dr. Hausser said as he walked around the desk and approached his guests. Thank you for coming to my island where history is about to be made. As he began walking toward the major, the major stood, placed his plate and drink on the side of the couch and slammed the heels of his shoes together, making a thunderous clapping sound. He raised his arm in a Hitler salute, which the doctor returned. "Major Hossteller and I have been developing this plan for over twenty years, correct?"

"Yes, Herr Doctor. A long time indeed. May I introduce Captain Albert Heilderman, my second in command." The Captain rose as the doctor approached, and like Major, he clicked his heels together and gave the Hitler salute.

"How do you do Captain. I have heard many wonderful things about your operations."

"Thank you, Herr Doctor," the Captain replied, clicking his heels again.

"Sadly, I only know these individuals by reputation. I have never met them personally," Hausser said, looking at the other three guests.

"This is Lt. Muller, and Sergeants Weber and Schneider," Major Hossteller said by way of introduction. Hausser studied their faces while shaking their hands.

"Gentlemen, so far I am impressed with the subjects you have collected for our study. The females have had all the physical characteristics I require. We have only had a 10% rejection rate, but that is something we cannot control. Your new assignment, which I will soon explain, is the key to our research. Everything rests of your shoulders," Hausser said, nodding up and down as he walked back to his desk and picked up the remote control. While doing so, he heard their heels clap together, and in his peripheral vision saw them raise their arms in a Hitler salute.

Hausser pressed a button on the remote that closed the expansive tapestry drapes, shutting off the inlet view and light, and consuming the room in darkness. Simultaneously, a giant swastika appeared on the large screen as Hausser began his PowerPoint presentation. Advancing the slide, a picture of Hitler replaced the swastika. All present quickly stood and shouted Heil Hitler as they saluted the screen. "Please gentlemen, be seated. We have much to discuss," Hausser said, motioning them to their seats.

An image appeared showing two large petri dishes 100 mm in diameter and 15mm in height, both lying on top of a black cloth covering a table. Inside the dishes were several teeth, and what appeared to be a large, slightly curved and thin section of bone.

"On December 26, 2018, the former Soviet Union displayed the teeth and bone fragments of our Fuhrer to the international press. At that time, Putin allowed French scientists to study this bone fragment and teeth to prove that, in fact, our Fuhrer died in 1945. They wanted the world to know that Herr Hitler died after taking cyanide and shooting himself in the head. Their research, published in the European Journal of Internal Medicine in May 2018, sought to once and for all end conspiracy theories about Adolf Hitler's death through scientific analysis of the teeth and skull."

"Those swine," Captain Albert Heilderman said. "Those that treat the Fuhrers' remains with such lack of respect should be hung by piano wire. Everyone voiced their agreement with him except Hausser who quietly advanced to the next slide.

"Their study proved that our Fuhrer died in 1945 and that the teeth were authentic beyond all doubt. Of course, for those of us present, we never doubted that our beloved Fuhrer took his own life in an honorable fashion.

"Though it's widely established that the Fuhrer died in his bunker in Berlin, rumors of his escape persist by conspiracy theorists. But this research (pointing to the screen) proves that he did not flee to Argentina in a submarine, he is not in a hidden base in Antarctica or on the dark side of the moon," Hausser said, holding back a laugh. (Slide advance) The new image showed a four-story building resembling a large hospital with an SS flag mounted over the entrance.

"This was the original Lebensborn in Munich. My grandfather, SS-Reichsführer Max Hausser was very instrumental in creating this breeding facility with the goal of raising the Aryan children birth rate. The children would be classified as racially pure and healthy based on our Nazi racial hygiene and health ideology at the time.

"You may not be aware that Lebensborn provided welfare to its mostly unmarried mothers. It encouraged anonymous births by unmarried women at their maternity homes, and mediated adoption of these children by likewise racially pure and healthy parents, particularly SS members and their

families. Females who bore the most Aryan children received this, (slide advance, showing a cross) the Cross of Honor of the German Mother. Those children who did not display the desired hereditary traits were disposed of, and in some cases if a particular female continued to give birth to undesirable offspring, they were eliminated as well.

"The program was expanded into several occupied European countries with Germanic populations during the Second World War. It included the selection of racially worthy orphans for adoption and care for children born from Aryan women who had been in relationships with SS members. It originally excluded children born from unions between common soldiers and foreign women because there was no proof of racial purity on both sides. During the war, many children were kidnapped from their parents and judged by Aryan criteria for their suitability to be raised in Lebensborn homes and fostered by German families.

"As you will see during your tour of my version of Lebensborn, we have taken Nazi eugenics to a whole new level. With females secured by Lt. Muller, Sergeants Weber and Schneider, our program has advanced at an accelerated rate. Most are doing well in our program as you shall see. Hormonal therapy has greatly aided in our research of viable donors carrying a fetus to full term. Sorry, I get carried away and tend to brag about our progress. Let us begin our tour gentlemen, and then we can return and discuss our next phase."

TWO

Following a short walk through a tropical floral trail leading away from the villa, Dr. Hausser and his quests reached a large multi-level facility closely resembling photographs of the original Lebensborn Hospital in Munich, even to the waving SS flag over the double-door entrance. The four-story building resembled a large mountain top retreat at first glance, the bottom story plastered in white stucco with numerous windows flanked by wooden shutters. The upper stories were clad in a wooden façade. A balcony finished with log rails wrapped around the entire second floor, and like the first level, it had numerous windows on all sides. The third and fourth floors also had log rail balconies extending from one corner of the front to the opposing corner.

Once inside the hospital, Dr. Hausser insisted that everyone don a white medical lab coat. Passing through three airlock doors, they entered a large gymnasium where twelve blond haired young women were playing badminton, paying little attention to those that had just entered. Most women wore their hair shoulder length or longer, and upon closer examination, all appeared to have ocean-blue eyes. None were twins, but their physical characteristics were remarkably similar.

"Please gentlemen, this way." Dr. Hausser led his guests to a bank of elevators, selecting one that took them to the floor above. "Here, I have to insist that you wear these medical masks to avoid passing on a possible pathogen to our donors." He handed each person a blue surgical mask, and once satisfied their mouths and noses were covered, he opened the elevator door to a large nursing station where five females dressed in blue scrubs were gathered.

"Good morning, ladies," Hausser said without expecting a reply. "Down these hallways, we have females who are undergoing our state-of-the-art hormonal therapy, allowing us to predict with 99% certainty when each female is ready for impregnation." Dr. Hausser laughed, and then caught himself. "I am sorry gentlemen, it is just that I am honored to inform you that when the famous Dolly the sheep was cloned in the 1996, the survival rate of the whole process was between 10%-20%. It took 277 tries to produce her. With our new technology, we have an 86% success rate.

"You see, it is not hard to clone a sheep or other animals, but cloning a human is a lot more complex. Aside from those who object to human cloning, their so-called ethical problem, the human component is much more complicated. Besides being dangerous, often ineffective, the reason for not experimenting in reproductive human cloning is that there are those in the medical field who question why it would be important to clone a human." Laughing again, he continued. "These are the same weaklings that scoff and denigrate what our predecessors in the SS accomplished both during the Lebensborn studies and during the important work conducted in our concentration camps, like my great-grandfather Dr. Mengele accomplished, but I digress.

"As I said, back in the late 1990s, it took scientists 277 tries to produce Dolly, their sheep. They pointed out that ethically studying the reproductive cloning of humans would require a large egg donor base in addition to a large number of surrogates to carry them."

"Added to these concerns, scientists that did consider human cloning discovered that some embryos expired before they could be implanted. Others resulted in miscarriages, and those making it to full-term soon died after birth due to abnormalities. Risks, they say, are easier to take with sheep than humans." Again, he began to laugh.

The group proceeded to a maternity ward where over 30 women were either holding or nursing newborns. "This is the result of our research. To date, we have produced over 137 Aryan children, but that is not enough. These children are given to various SS officers throughout the world, but that is not the main purpose of our research here on the island. I will explain later, but all in good time."

"How many do you plan to produce, Herr Doctor?" asked Lt. Muller.

"Ah, it is not about how many more Aryan children we can produce. No, it is about who we can produce. Come gentlemen, you must be famished. Let us head back to the villa for lunch."

After everyone filled their plates, Dr. Hausser returned to his desk and turned on his Mac computer again. "This is Lubyanka Square in the Meshchansky District of Moscow. It is the popular name for the FSB headquarters, the Russian secret police."

The screen displayed a massive building. "The Russians have preserved and protected our Fuhrer's remains in this building." Hausser could hear mumbling from a few behind him. "We now believe we know the exact location of these items (again pointing to the screen showing teeth and a portion of a skull cap) and the job for you, Lt. Muller, Sergeant Weber, and Sergeant Schneider, is to steal them." The three looked at each other but said nothing.

He then opened the middle desk drawer, removed a large envelope, and handed it to Lt. Muller. "This is all the material we have gathered to date about the FSB headquarters and the floor containing the Fuhrer's remains. I would be remiss if I did not remind you that this is top secret, and if you feel the need to use other contractors to complete your mission, they must be eliminated at your conclusion." Muller acknowledged that he understood and returned to his seat.

"Without being too technical, we will harvest our leader's DNA from these items, and through our latest breakthroughs in genetics and cloning, we will resurrect the Fuhrer and start the Fourth Reich." Everyone jumped to attention. Shouts of Sieg Heil, Sieg Heil, Sieg Heil filled the room to Dr. Hausser's delight.

After basking in the applause, Hausser raised his hand and requested silence. "Each of you should be proud of being selected by The Organization to participate in this historic program. Through your successful efforts, your names will forever be praised by the Fourth Reich."

Following a hardy seafood and freshly baked bread lunch, the guests returned to the dock and departed in their respective sea planes. Hausser took a long cool shower, feeling satisfied with his presentation. Everything was progressing as scheduled. Putting on a fresh set of white trousers and shirt, he slipped on his sandals and walked to the rear of the residence. As he continued to the adjacent hospital through the long winding path flanked by heavy tropical vegetation, the air filled with the sounds of tropical birds and buzzing insects.

Upon entering the hospital, he removed a white lab coat from the coat rack and slipped it on, then took out a surgical mask from his right front pocket and attached it to his ears. A female nurse approached and greeted him. "Herr Doctor, your patients are waiting," she said while handing him a metal clipboard holding a stack of papers containing patient records. He glanced at them and started his walk down the long hallway accompanied by the nurse.

"Any problems I should be aware of?" he asked.

"Nein, everyone seems to be doing well with the new hormones, Herr Doctor."

"Everyone is ovulating as charted?" he asked.

"Ja, Herr Doctor."

"Wunderbar, everything is going splendidly. Soon, we will have the only missing element to conclude our experiment. When I have the items in my possession, we can proceed."

THREE

THREE WEEKS LATER

Lt. Muller, Sergeant Weber, and Sergeant Schneider sat separately during their flight to Moscow, arriving 15-minutes earlier than scheduled. They were careful not to make noticeable contact at the luggage area and departed the Sheremetyevo Alexander S. Pushkin International Airport in separate taxis destined for different hotels. They had plans to meet the following morning at a restaurant in Lubyanka Square in downtown Moscow near the former KGB and now FSB headquarters. The FSB's main responsibilities within Russia included counter-intelligence, internal and border security, counter-terrorism and surveillance, as well as to investigate other types of grave crimes and federal law violations that most Russians suspected, but never questioned.

Muller was the first to arrive at the medium sized eatery and requested a table near a window overlooking a large building across the street. Looking at the large four-story building, he patted his breast pocket to make sure he still had the documents he would share with the other two men when they arrived.

Weber arrived first, followed 30-seconds later by Schneider. Both spotted Muller who gave an all-clear wave, meaning it was safe to approach his table. They placed their orders with the waitress who immediately returned with two coffees and one tea. As soon as she left, Weber removed the documents from his pocket and spread them on the table. "The Lubyanka actually consists of three buildings, but this yellow building is the main building. It contains the Federal Security Service (FSB) Directorate and our items.

"Believe it or not, the Russians conduct tours of this building, including its KGB museum. The ground floor next to the museum is used for conferences and has a clubroom for retired KGB officers. It features a disco, among other things. The upper floors contain offices for FSB agents, and this room (pointing to the map) is where the safe is located. Today, each of us will take a tour of the museum at different times, gathering as much information as possible without drawing attention to ourselves. We'll meet back here at 5:00 p.m. for dinner and discuss how we might proceed."

At 5:00 p.m., the three SS officers met again at the restaurant as planned. "This will not be easy," Weber said. "There is heavy security posted at the entrance near the elevator that leads to the second floor, and I assume others are present when the lift arrives on the floors above." Muller and Schneider confirmed this was what they observed or suspected.

"Not only that," Weber said, "You can bet there are alarms in the room containing the vault, not to mention the vault itself." No one spoke for a few minutes, sipping their cocktails while glancing outside at the growing crowd approaching the building.

Lt. Muller was the first to break the silence. "I think we all agree that more intelligence is needed before we can devise an action plan. I will contact The Organization and request more operatives familiar with the building layout and get the information we need. Tomorrow, do your own thing. Check out the city. Act as tourists. I will ring your rooms once I have new information and we can reconvene here."

The next day after meeting for breakfast, Muller and Weber joined Schneider in his rented SUV. Muller told them he had received an email from The Organization that included a photo of Lana Zagitova, a single 34-year-old mother of one. He showed them the photo--a striking Russian woman, 5'2" with long black hair and high cheek bones. She could easily be a top model in other countries; but is Russia, she did not stand out among the many other beautiful women.

The Organization's only information after tailing Zagitova was that she worked in some capacity for the FSB and always took the elevator to its second-floor headquarters. What service she provided on that floor was unknown, but she was the only possible source for learning the in-and-outs of that particular section of the building. They were also given her last known address. The day's goal was to locate her apartment and get the lay of the land. Early the following morning, Weber would begin tailing her from that location to the FSB headquarters. Using handheld radios instead of cellphones, Weber would inform Muller when she arrived so he could station himself discretely near the elevators to see if she indeed headed to the second floor.

At 6:50 a.m. the following morning, Zagitova left her apartment and caught a bus on the corner by her complex in route to the FSB. At her stop, she exited and headed directly to the headquarters building, unaware of the man wearing a trench coat and holding an umbrella in the lobby watching her enter. Once inside he saw her take the elevator and saw from the lighted floor indicator, that it stopped on the second floor.

Later, the three men met at a local cafe at 7:50 a.m. and took seats in the back. While waiting for their coffees to arrive, they discussed what they had seen and what they should do next.

One thing that Weber and Muller liked about SS officer Schneider was that he always allowed them to make suggestions. Sometimes he accepted them as offered, and at other times he did not; in the latter case, he offered what he thought was a better plan. If their opinions were dismissed, he had at least given them a chance to express themselves. That night was no different. After listening to their input and agreeing with many of their suggestions, Schneider outlined his own plan for the following evening.

"Herr Doctor, patient 147 is in labor," a nurse said to Hausser as he arrived for his evening rounds.

"Good. It is about time. I will meet you in surgery." He went to the outer door of the surgery ward and began sterilizing his hands before accepting assistance from a second nurse who helped him put on his gloves and mask. Keeping his arms in the air, he walked into the surgery room where he saw a female in the throes of birthing. Even though these pregnancies were considered high risk, Hausser was calm in his demeanor--never addressing the woman lying on a table with her feet in stirrups. Hausser looked at the monitors showing the heart rates of both the mother and fetus. He found that going the epidural route was the best way to proceed.

A catheter was attached after the epidural shot was administered. He noted that the contractions were becoming extremely intense and close together and that she was now dilated to 10 centimeters. It was time. After seven commands to push, the infant's head started to appear. Since this was patient 147's third delivery, the birth canal was wide enough to preclude forceps usage. Immediately, Dr. Hausser saw the infant's deformed head. He glanced at the surgical nurse who also saw it. Without a command, the nurse grabbed the oxygen mask and placed it on the woman's face. Flipping a switch from oxygen to another source, she told the patient to breathe deeply. The infant was draped in a sheet and placed on the women's chest.

Hausser nodded to the nurse who turned on the gas, as Dr. Hausser moved to the woman's side. She started to gasp and thrash but was held down by both the nurse and Hausser. Approximately 20 seconds later she stopped moving and expired. The nurse quickly shut off the monitoring equipment and removed the oxygen mask.

"What is it that the Americans always say?" asked Hausser. He then answered himself, "Oh, yes. Win some, lose some. Take them away and tell Joseph I need him as well as Hinrich and Ewin to be at the dormitory tonight at precisely 2300 hours. I want you here at 2200 so we can take care of the subjects no longer needed. Ten females are all we need."

"Yes, Herr Doctor. I will tell them and see you here at 2200 hours."

The baby continued to cry on the chest of the deceased surrogate. After removing all monitoring tubes from the body, the nurse quickly wheeled the gurney through the ward to the exiting doors and on to the bank of elevators where she was greeted by Joseph, the male intern, when the elevator door opened. He took control of the gurney, and after backing inside the elevator, pushed the basement button and waited for the doors to close.

Reaching the basement, he pushed the gurney toward a commercial grade cremation chamber. Opening the chamber door, he pushed the deceased surrogate into the oven with the infant still on her chest. He closed the door, and using a digital command pad, heard a blast of gas followed by leaping flames engulfing the chamber, overcoming the brief cry of the infant.

After washing up, Dr. Hausser entered notes into patient 147's record. The notes reflected two prior births which resulted in two other deaths. The first was stillborn followed by a second that lived two days before dying of organ malformations. With an unending supply of viable surrogates, he had no time for unhealthy females. The Fourth Reich depended on his success.

FOUR

"Guten morgen," Dr. Hausser said to the nursing staff he had assembled in the large hospital meeting room the following morning. "Last night, I received great news. Great news! Soon we will have the remains of our great leader, Adolf Hitler, in our possession." Several nurses began clapping and some cried, soon to be joined in elation by everyone else in the room.

"In addition, we will soon be receiving the second to last surrogate. This means we must quickly isolate the DNA from our Fuhrer's remains so that impregnation can begin in a few weeks."

He looked at his surgical go-to nurse. "How is the indoctrination program going with the other subjects?"

"Fine, Herr Doctor. We did have to eliminate one who continually fought the process and attempted numerous escapes, but now we have eight fully ingrained with the ideals of National Socialism. I expect our newest subject to arrive the day after tomorrow, and her processing will begin then. Assuming the tenth subject arrives within the next two weeks, we will be ready for impregnation."

"Wunderbar. Ladies, we are on the threshold of a glorious new world order. An order that was envisioned by our Fuhrer, but the world was not prepared to adopt it. Now, with our advances in human cloning, a world ruled by the Aryan race is near."

At 6:00 p.m. Lana Zagitova was observed leaving the FSB building and boarding a bus for home. Exiting twenty minutes later, she entered a corner grocery store and emerged with a full bag of groceries--a short walk from there, and she was home. Her apartment building was built during the Stalin days, and as the old American song by Malvina Reynold, Little Boxes, suggested, they all looked alike. Americans who visit large Russian cities refer to them as "Stalin boxes."

Living in a building without an elevator, she was thankful her apartment was on the second floor, particularly since she had a young child. She opened her flat and placed the bag of groceries on the kitchen counter, then went downstairs to her neighbor's unit to retrieve her child, not noticing the man standing by the building's entrance. Once more with her son in her arms, she climbed back upstairs and pushed her door open. Her son was starting to awaken from a nap, so she placed him on the couch and went back to the front door to hang up her coat.

She heard a soft knock on her door and thought that perhaps it was her neighbor bringing something she had left behind when she picked up her son. As soon as she began opening the door, it slammed into her face cutting her upper lip. Confused, she saw and felt a knife placed on her throat while the man holding it told her not to scream. A second man entered the apartment and closed the door. The man with the knife directed her to a chair. He pulled out two zip ties and secured her hands to the back of the seat. Next, he took a cloth gag and put it in her mouth after wiping away blood from her lip.

Saying something to the other man in German, he put the knife back in his pocket and glanced over at the boy who had fallen back to sleep. Grabbing another chair and turning it around, he sat across from Lana. In broken Russian he told her they did not want to hurt her or her son. Tears rolled down her cheeks. He told her to stop crying. She tried but was unsuccessful.

The second man emptied the contents of Lana's purse on the kitchen table and placed her cell phone in his pants pocket. Rummaging through the remaining items, he bypassed the cash and loose change and took an identification card that had a clip at the top for attaching to one's clothing. He knew it was the identification card for the FSB. Lana looked at him as if questioning what this was all about.

The man who had held the knife said something to his partner who went into the small kitchen looking for coffee and a pot. Not finding any, he said something to the other who again, in poor Russian, asked Lana where the coffee was. She tried to respond, but the gag prevented it. He again brandished the knife and told her that if she screamed, he would kill her son. She nodded, at which point he removed the gag from her mouth, but kept it tied behind her neck. She told him where it was in Russian, pointing to where she stored the coffee. The second man opened the cupboard, found it, and made a pot.

"What do you want?" she asked. "I don't have much money, but what I have you can take. Please leave me and my son alone. We have done nothing to you."

While his partner brewed coffee in the kitchen, the man placed the knife on the table and leaning forward. "We are not here for your money, and like I said, we do not want to harm you. Instead, we want you to do a simple task for us tomorrow. That's all. One simple task."

"What simple task?" she asked, trying to control her crying.

"All in good time. Are you a good cook? You must prepare food for me, my friend and your son who will wake up soon, no doubt. Do not try anything or Herr Vogel (holding a gun) will shoot your son." She nodded and waited for him to untie her. Once freed of the zip ties which he simply cut off, she pulled her hands from behind her and began massaging them. Picking up the knife, he motioned for her to join his partner in the kitchen who lustfully looked her over and smiled.

Twenty minutes later, she placed boiled potatoes, meat and cheese on the kitchen table. A plate with black bread was the last item offered to the men. She was told to sit in a chair between them, blocking any avenue of escape while they ate. She refused food. As the men finished their meal, her son began to stir on the couch. She attempted to stand, but Vogel grabbed her breast and pushed her back onto the chair.

"You will tell your son that we are friends from work, OK? You will feed him and do your normal nightly routine with him, but if we suspect you are trying to escape, he will be the first to die. Do you understand?"

"Da," Lana said as she waited for Vogel to release her breast. As he did, he stood and pushed back his chair, allowing her to walk to the couch. Her son sat up and immediately asked who the men were. She made up a short story about how she worked with them and had invited them over for dinner as she walked him to the kitchen and had him sit down to eat. She plated a dish for him and poured some juice. Neither man spoke, allowing Lana to communicate with her son without interference. After dinner, she told the men it was time to give her son a bath. The one who had held the knife acknowledged this by turning toward the bathroom. As Lana and her son made it to the bathroom, she saw Vogel standing in the hallway. There was nowhere for her and her son to go.

After the son's bath, Lana put him in bed and read a story from a children's book. A few minutes later he was sound asleep. She returned to the kitchen where she was directed to take a seat at the table.

"Lana, we know you work for the FSB. We also know that you work on the second floor of the FSB headquarters." The man who had held the knife pulled out a roughly drawn map of the building she worked in and asked, "How many people work on the second floor?"

"I don't really know," she said which resulted in an unexpected slap across her face from Vogel. The blow caused her lip to bleed again, but no offer was made to help her clean it up.

"Lana. You are a beautiful woman with a handsome son. You do not want my friend there to scar up such a pretty face before cutting off one of your son's fingers, do you?"

Lana began to cry and shook her head no. "Please, do what you want to me, but leave my son alone."

"That is entirely up to you isn't it, Lana? Now, let's try this again. How many people work on the second floor?"

"The floor is divided into several sections. Some have two to three people working in each one while other departments may have 10-15 people. Altogether, maybe 40-45 people each day."

"See, that was nothard, was it? Now, where on the second floor is the safe containing our Fuhrer's remains?"

Lana's face showed shock. These were Nazis intent on stealing their dead leader's teeth and whatever else was in the safe that she had never seen in her many years with the FSB.

"What? What do you mean?" she asked, resulting in another blow from Vogel, but this time to the back of her head.

"I think she needs to be a little more comfortable, don't you?" Vogel asked. He told Lana to stand, which she did, but she did not face him. From behind, he grabbed the front of her blouse and tore it open, ripping off several buttons in the process. She attempted to grab the remnants of the blouse, but in one motion her bra was cut from behind and removed. She was then forcefully shoved back onto her chair. Covering both her breasts, she began to cry.

"Lana. Why do you want to make my friend so angry? We are not here to harm you. One simple task. That is all that we want you to do, and then we will leave." After she composed herself, he pointed at the map again. "Which room has the safe we are interested in?"

Trying as best she could to cover up both breasts with one hand and arm, she pointed to a small east room on the second floor. "The safe with Hitler's remains is here, but only a few have the combination. I don't have it." She thought she would receive another blow from Vogel, but it never came.

"No, but we expect you to get the combination and retrieve the articles we want from it. Do as we ask, and we will be out of your life. You will never see either of us again." They threw more questions at her regarding the room's setup, security cameras, and the number of personnel in it. Lana finally admitted that she and her supervisor were the only ones at that part of the building and that there were no security cameras in the office. The FSB management thought that the metal detector, security officers, and security cameras focused on the elevators were all that was needed.

"Tonight, you will call your neighbor and tell her that friends are visiting from out of town and they will be spending some time with you, and that there will be no need for her to babysit your son tomorrow. Tomorrow morning, you will feed your son as normal, give him something to occupy his time, and then head to work. You will be watched the whole time, so do not alert anyone. If you do, your son will be dead by the time you get home.

At work, you will obtain the items we want and secure the safe. If we suspect that an alarm has been activated or you have alerted someone, he will die." He then looked at Vogel, who in turn told Lana to get ready for bed.

Lana stood and headed for her bedroom with Vogel in tow. Her son was deeply asleep in his bed. "You need to take a shower," he told her. He walked her to the bathroom. She attempted to close the door, but he held it open with his foot and had a smile on his face. Turning away from him, she undressed and climbed into the shower, pulling the vinyl curtain closed. When finished she dried herself off and put on a flannel top and matching pants. She quickly walked past the onlooker and climbed into bed with her son, placing her arm over him.

Sleep under the circumstances was impossible. She opened her eyes a little to see if she were still being watched, but found she was alone; however, the bedroom door was open. A quiet conversation was taking place in the kitchen. She could not make out what was being said. It all transpired in German.

FIVE

At 5:00 a.m., Lana was awakened by the man who had held the knife to her throat the day before. "It's time for you to get ready," he said, pulling back the blanket and comforter that covered her, but leaving the portion of blanket covering her son who was still sound asleep. "Let him sleep. It will be over soon, so why disturb him. How long does it take you to get ready for work?"

Before she could answer, Vogel entered the room carrying two cups of coffee. He gave one to his partner and the other to Lana. "Less than an hour normally, but since I do not have to take care of Maxim, it should be shorter," Lana finally replied.

"Good. You will leave at your normal time and catch the bus you use each day. Go now and take a shower and put on your makeup. My partner here will make us some breakfast." No one followed her to the bathroom this time. With no phone and no window in the bathroom, escape was impossible.

After showering and putting on a dark pantsuit, she gave her son a kiss on his forehead and walked to the kitchen. A plate with a boiled potato and scrambled egg with toast was on the table. When she did not touch her food, Vogel told her to eat. "I am not hungry," she said. He started to raise his hand to hit her, but she quickly grabbed her coffee and said that she normally has only coffee or tea and a piece of toast. That reply seemed to satisfy him.

The time for her to leave the apartment was upon them. Intruder number one had her stand up while he examined her attire, then he took a broach from his pocket and pinned it to the lapel of her suit jacket. "Do not remove this piece of jewelry. It will show us what you are doing and saying. If you try to tell someone or do something stupid, we will know, and your son will be killed. Do you understand?"

"Da," she said, as tears began to build in her eyes.

"Do not cry," said Vogel. "You do not want to mess up your makeup."

Lana asked if she could kiss her son goodbye one more time before leaving and her request was honored, but she was watched by both men. Intruder number one showed Lana a handgun that he placed in the front pocket of his trench coat as they headed for the front door. "Soon, this will be all over and you and Maxim will be lying on your couch together with no cares of the world."

Vogel opened the apartment door, allowing Lana to leave first followed by his partner. Reaching street level, he motioned for her to proceed toward the bus. Once she stepped inside, he got into his car and followed. Opening a laptop set on the passenger seat and typing a few strokes, he clearly saw the interior of the bus through the broach's lens. The video was in high-def color with outstanding audio. "You have to congratulate the Americans for their technology," he said out loud, making sure he followed the bus closely.

The bus stopped about 200 yards from the FSB building. Lana did not turn to see if she could spot her kidnapper. She walked briskly to her place of employment, thinking only of her son. Entering the building, she and made her way through the metal detector without setting it off. Two uniformed officers at the entrance did not bother to look up as she passed; they not only recognized her but saw her approach the building on their security screens.

The kidnappers were not concerned about the broach setting off the metal detector since the only metal in the jewelry was a small battery.

Lana pushed the second-floor call button and stared at the door, finding the elevator empty when it opened. She entered and pressed the button for the second-floor. Once in her office, she found that her supervisor had not arrived yet. The safe was in a small, almost closet-like room only a few feet from her desk. She entered it and looked at the safe, knowing the person observing her outside the building would be interested in seeing it. Lana returned to her desk, still trying to devise a plan that would get her supervisor to open the safe. It was hard for her to focus, thinking of her son awaking and only seeing a strange man in their apartment.

SIX

Lana was startled and jumped when her supervisor, Andrii, finally arrived and greeted he. "Dobroye Utro." She returned his greeting and smiled at him. He had shown interest in her in the past and she hoped he still felt that way. He was married and had two children but had confided in her on numerous occasions that he and his wife had drifted apart and were no longer in an intimate marriage. In the past, when he brought the subject up, she kiddingly suggested he contact an escort service. His reply was always the same: "On my salary?"

"So, how was your night?" he asked. Each day started with his same question.

"Actually, last night I watched a documentary on Adolf Hitler's death in his bunker. It was one of those shows where the hosts were trying to convince viewers that Hitler had been secretly snuck out of Germany and a body double was actually killed and cremated."

Andrii laughed. "Sometimes people, especially Americans, have to have a conspiracy angle for everything," he replied. "I have seen and heard similar programs. Hitler was transported to Argentina on a

German U-boat, or he was flown to Brazil. Those people are so stupid."

With her back toward Andrii, Lana unbuttoned three buttons of her blouse, showing not only her cleavage, but her lacy black bra. She turned to Andrii in such a way that he had to notice her exposure. "You know, Andrii, when I watched that program, I realized that in all the years I have worked here, you have never shown me Hitler's remains." The whole time she spoke, Andrii's eyes focused on her breasts. Still seated, she maneuvered her chair in such a way that her knees were now touching his. "Maybe someday you will show me, da?" she said while placing her left hand on his upper thigh. She could see he was getting an erection.

"Yes, I think that can be arranged," he said, waiting for his erection to subside. Lana got up and poured herself a cup of tea, feeling his eyes on her every move. Getting out of his chair, he took her arm and escorted her to the safe room. "Why not now?" he said, closing the door and walking to the safe. Obviously paying little attention to the combination he was entering, she strategically placed her cup of tea close to the safe.

Opening the safe, he carefully removed two round plastic dishes, similar to petri dishes she had seen before, and put them on the counter where Lana had placed her tea. Without opening the dishes, he told her the story of how the FSB came into possession of the items. Acting interested, Lana inserted her right hand inside her blouse as if she were excited about seeing the items.

Andrii's attention turned from the two dishes to Lana's cleavage, surprising her by pulling her toward him. She could feel his erection getting larger. He wanted to remove her jacket, but fully aware the broach could not be laid aside, she unhooked the clip at the front of her bra, exposing herself. She grabbed his hand that was trying to slip off her jacket and put it on one of her breasts, then she took off his tie, turned him around, and placed the tie over his eyes, tying in behind his head. Turning back, he began fondling her breasts. She pushed him to a small table next to the safe and began opening the buttons on his shirt while pulling it free from his trousers. She then undid his belt buckle, pulled his trousers and briefs to the ground and began kissing his manhood, occasionally inserting it into her mouth. He arched his back in ecstasy.

"Do not go anywhere," she whispered. "I need to get a sip of tea." Silently, she grabbed the two dishes and placed them in her jacket and closed the safe. She purposely made a low slurping sound and went back to his erection. "I put those items back in the safe and closed it. Now we can concentrate on pleasing each other." She pulled down her pants and panties and mounted her supervisor, bringing him to an early climax.

When finished and returning to relaxed breathing, they redressed with few words exchanged. Lana finished first but waited for Andrii. Once redressed, he walked to the safe. Lana's heart leaped for fear he might reopen it and discover the theft. Instead, he simply spun the dial and they left the safe room together.

They returned to their respective desks without exchanging glances. Finally, Andrii broke the silence by saying, "Spasibo." Lana smiled at him and returned the thank you. When lunch time arrived, Lana left the building as usual to grab something to eat from a street vendor and go for a walk. This day, however, she immediately headed for the bus stop and took the first available bus headed toward her apartment. Upon arrival and stepping onto the pavement, she was surprised to find the kidnapper waiting for her. She started to reach into her jacket pocket for the items he wanted when he said, "Not here. Wait until we get inside your apartment."

At her door, the kidnapper rapped on it using a patterned sequence and Vogel opened it from the inside. Lana quickly ran to her son who was playing with toys on the floor in front of the television and hugged him. She then stood and pulled out the two dishes and handed them to Vogel. "You two have what you want, so now leave us."

The second intruder said, "Yes. You did an excellent job, Lana, and I think your supervisor was very happy with your performance. I know I enjoyed watching it," He turned his back to her for a moment, and when he turned back, she saw the gun which now had a suppressor attached. Before she could react, he shot her once in the head and twice in the chest. Her son saw his mother's blouse turn a scarlet red before he, too, was shot in the head. His partner lifted Lana's limp body and laid it on the couch and placed her son next to her. Placing a blanket over them, the two left. "On the couch with your son. That is what I promised."

Three evenings later, a seaplane arrived in the cove where the doctor was waiting at the dock. Looking at his driver and bodyguards, he announced, "Gentlemen, you are witnessing history." Two males exited once the plane was it was securely tied to the mooring. One carrying a briefcase. "Heil Hitler," they both said while giving the Nazi salute.

"Heil Hitler indeed," Hausser replied. "Please, let me hold the briefcase." He immediately pressed it firmly to his chest and held it there as he was driven back to the villa. A second car carrying the two visitors who had just arrived tailed his limo.

"Gentlemen, you must be tired from your trip and hungry. Please, pour yourself a drink and Rosa will ready a buffet for you. I will return after locking your valuable cargo in my safe. Excusing himself, he climbed the stairs to his study and carefully placed the briefcase on his desk. Once the safe was opened, he drew in a deep breath and removed the two plastic dishes from the briefcase. He first inspected the vial containing a portion of human skull with a wound on the left side and black charring, consistent with a gunshot wound from close range. The other dish contained a partial dental bridge and four misshapen teeth, brown at the base and a small tarter deposit still visible after nearly a century.

Wiping a tear from his left eye, he said out loud, "Mein Fuhrer." He placed the containers side-by-side on the first shelf of the safe and closed the door thinking that soon, the world will not be without the greatest leader of the 20th Century.

SEVEN

14 MONTHS LATER

"Tell me again why we're going to the airport," Ismail asked Jeannie who was driving her bureau Crown Vic. An eighteen-year veteran FBI agent, Ismail had worked with his supervisor, Assistant Special Agent in Charge, Jeannie Loomis, for the past 10 years. Considering her more a friend than supervisor or colleague, he loved to verbally harass her anytime he got the chance.

"The TSA at SFO requested us after detaining a guy they called a wacko trying to quickly reclaim his luggage and exit the terminal," Jeannie answered. "When they asked him what he had hidden in large tubes designed to carry things like documents, or you know, architectural designs, he tried to run. After they caught him and cleared out the baggage area, they called the bomb squad. Now this will creep you out. The tubes didn't have any bomb making material, they were filled with small jars of spiders."

"Spiders! God, I hate spiders! What the hell was he doing with spiders, and why do we have to respond? Maybe they should request animal control instead of us elite FBI agents," Ismail said.

"Will you stop? You're such a big baby. You face down armed gunmen, stop terrorists from committing acts of mass destruction, and you're afraid of little spiders," Jeannie said with a big smile. The fact was that she and Ismail had recently tracked down and gotten into a shootout at the San Francisco Zoo, an altercation that ended in the death of a serial cop killer. Prior to that incident, they stopped three jihadists from blowing up the underwater BART (Bay Area Rapid Transit) tube connecting San Francisco to Oakland.

"Hey, did you ever see that movie Kingdom of the Spiders with William Shatner?" Ismail asked. "Hundreds of thousands of spiders suddenly became aggressive and started killing people in Arizona."

"No. Don't remember seeing that one," Jeannie responded.

"You never saw that?" Ismail asked. "Damn, at the end of the movie, Shatner's house was covered with so many spider webs, he couldn't get out. Gives me shivers to just think about it."

"Are you through?" Jeannie asked. "God, I can't take you anywhere. All we need to do is interview the perv and ask what the hell he was doing with the spiders. That's all. Will you be okay with that, or should I leave you in the car?"

"Well, okay if that's all we're going to do. Do you think we might have time to buy a Cinnabon while we're there?" Ismail asked.

Jeannie parked in the "Reserved for Law Enforcement" parking slot and walked to security with Ismail in tow. They showed the attending TSA agent their identification and were escorted into a long hallway with offices on each side. "This is where he is," the agent said, returning to his desk.

"The spiders aren't there, are they?" Ismail called out, but he did not get a reply.

"Get in here," Jeannie said. "What the hell do you do at home when you find a big bad spider?"

"That's what the wifey and kids are for. There's no need for a highly trained FBI agent such as moi to get involved," Ismail replied.

"God, what does your wife see in you?" Jeannie commented.

"Hey, as I've told you before, she looks at me and sees all this USDA prime sex machine and she can't resist." Jeannie shook her head and saw another male TSA agent walking toward them. "

FBI?" he asked.

"Yes," came Jeannie's reply as she held out her badge.

"He's down the hallway."

"And the spiders?" Ismail asked, getting a death ray stare from Jeannie.

"They're in a separate room with some college professor. The guy's name is Melcum Williams, an

Australian. His flight originated in Sydney. As far as we can tell, the motive is all greed. Here's the room," the agent said as he opened a locked door using a large set of keys on a ring. He allowed Jeannie and Ismail to enter before following them inside a larger than expected interview room.

Melcum Williams looked to be in his early thirties with blond hair and the start of a mustache. A twelve-o'clock shadow had taken over his face during the long flight. Jeannie looked at Ismail who took that as a request to start the interrogation.

"Mr. Williams, I'm Special Agent Flores of the FBI and this is my supervisor, Agent Loomis."

"FBI! Oh my God, I'm not a terrorist. I'm just a guy trying to make some extra cash, that's all." Before Ismail could start his line of questioning, there was a knock on the door and a female TSA agent stepped in, requesting to talk to the TSA agent with them. The agent got up, excused himself, and shut the door on his way out.

"Let's start again," Ismail said. "Your name is Malcum or Melcem Willliams and you're an Australian, is that correct?"

"Yes, that's correct," came the reply.

"Let me cut to the chase. What the hell were you doing with a bunch of spiders on the plane?" Ismail had barely finished his question when the interview room door opened and the TSA agent motioned to Jeannie and Ismail that he would like to talk with them outside.

Exiting the room, Jeannie and Ismail saw a thin female who appeared to be in her sixties and in dire need of a hair and makeup appointment. The TSA agent looked at the woman and introduced her. "This is Professor Paula Stronberg from Stanford University. She specializes in spiders."

"Actually, when I'm out of the classroom people call me Doctor Stronberg. I'm an arachnologist." Greetings were exchanged and Jeannie could see that Ismail was having a hard time hiding his irritation over Dr. Stronberg's egotistic demeanor.

"So, Doctor Stronberg, what type of spiders are we talking about?" Jeannie asked before Ismail could become snarky.

"I have never seen so many Atrax Robustus together at one time. I counted over 200 specimens," she answered.

"And what are Atrax Robustus?" Ismail asked, almost clenching his teeth while posing the question.

"Sorry. Of course. Atrax Robustus in the common layman term for a class of extremely venomous spiders called the Sydney Funnel Web that are native to eastern Australia, usually found within a one-hundred kilometer, or sixty-two mile radius of Sydney. Its bite, and the male is the most toxic, can cause serious illness or death in humans if untreated. Its body length ranges from one to five centimeters, that's roughly one-half to two inches, and both sexes are glossy and darkly colored, ranging from blue-black, to black, to shades of brown or dark-plum. This individual has a great collection of both sexes."

"They typically build silk-lined tubular burrow retreats with collapsed tunnels or open tunnel entrances from which irregular trip-lines radiate over the ground. There are exceptions which lack trip-lines and may have trapdoors. The silk entrance tube may be split into two openings, in a Y or T form. The spiders burrow in sheltered habitats where they can find a moist and humid environment. For instance, they're often found under rocks, logs or borer holes in rough-barked trees. They're basically ambush predators."

God, will she ever shut up, Ismail thought to himself. Jeannie interrupted the lecture by asking Stronberg why she thought the suspect was transporting them to the United States.

"Oh, that's an elementary question young lady." Jeannie wanted to smack her but allowed the urge to pass.

"You see, there's a thriving black market for deadly funnel-web spiders and tarantulas. They're being bought and sold online and there's nothing the Australian authorities can do to stop it. I heard that a person was recently caught trying to transport Inland Taipans, nasty snakes, and if they ever got loose on a plane...," she shook her head. "Come to think of it, if those spiders somehow got loose..." She stopped and paused before continuing.

"Adult tarantulas are being sold on the Gumtree shopping site for up to a hundred and eighty dollars, and you can purchase Funnel-web spiders for sixty dollars and up. The funnel-webs this gentleman was transporting would net him a considerable profit, depending on how much he had to originally pay for them. But if he collected them himself, well, you do the math. He had over two-hundred Funnel-webs in those tubes. By the way, before you ask, each of these spiders have venom strong enough to kill a human in minutes."

"Who would want to purchase venomous spiders?" Jeannie asked.

"Labs, universities, maybe clinics," Dr. Stronberg answered. "They harvest the venom and sell it to make antivenom, but I highly doubt you'll find any records of these transactions. I mean, some of these spiders and snakes are on the endangered species list, and although I doubt a person would receive any real incarceration time, it would certainly put a black mark against any institution of higher learning. With that in mind, what do you think will happen to these specimens?"

"I say, kill them," Ismail blurted out.

"Oh, heaven's no!" Dr. Stronberg responded. "They need to be cared for and studied. Their venom is very valuable in the creation of antivenom. Please, can you possibly talk to the individual who will be making that decision and recommend that Stanford University be considered?"

Nothing earth shattering was learned during the Williams interrogation. He did provide the names of labs and his contacts. As Dr. Stromberg surmised, he collected the specimens himself in the wild and already had contacts with three labs in the San Francisco Bay area that would pay him eighty to one-hundred dollars per specimen. Jeannie would check with SAC Lomax to see who had jurisdiction from this point forward. It would come down to Williams' statement and the probable denial by individual labs. He was booked for the unlawful transportation of endangered species. Jeannie would let legal decide what else could be tacked on but did include in her report that Williams cooperated with them, giving them needed information on labs and the identification of those who would now be investigated. She got permission from the SAC to transfer the Funnel-webs into the custody of Dr. Stronberg and Stanford University. Both were thrilled with their new arachnid collection.

Jeannie rewarded Ismail for not blowing his cool with Dr. Stronberg by buying him a Cinnabon and small coffee at the airport. They smelled so good she could not resist buying one for herself. They found an empty table near the Cinnabon concession stand and ate there. "Tell me you didn't think of that movie, Snakes on the Plane, when that condescending doctor talked about the possibility of the spiders escaping those tubes," Ismail said.

"Yeah, I thought of that as soon as she mentioned it. Thank God each spider was in an individual container. But still, and I have to admit, it gave me the creeps," Jeannie replied.

"Who's the big baby now?" Ismail said with a grin as he began stuffing the last of the Cinnabon into his mouth.

EIGHT

At 10 p.m., Dr. Hausser was back in the hospital whistling Wagner's Ride of the Valkyries while putting on his lab coat. He was soon joined by surgical nurse Frau Becker. "They have all been sedated?" he asked.

"Yes," Herr Doctor. "To avoid suspicion, everyone is sleeping in their normal bed, included those chosen."

"Good. Now we do what must be done." He briefly left the room and returned with a tray containing several syringes and bottles of pancuronium bromide, potassium chloride, and sodium thiopental. "We can thank the Americans for their hard work in deciding what chemicals are humanly necessary to carry out death penalties in the United States." He approached the first bed and had his nurse verify that the subject was slated for termination. "Yes, Herr Doctor."

Hausser placed the needle in the first bottle, and after taking a measured dose, did the same from the other two. He then found a vein and injected the deadly cocktail into the sleeping victim. "Thank you for your service to the Fourth Reich," he said, as he proceeded down the line of beds to the next one.

Eight females would be allowed to sleep and wake naturally, but twelve had served their purpose for the Aryan race.

After administering the last deadly injection, he sent Frau Becker to get coffee for them both. They sat at a table at the far end of the dormitory and talked and laugh about nothing important. Finally, three male interns arrived, each pushing a gurney.

"Gentlemen. I must apologize for not telling you how important your work is for The Organization and the future of the National Socialist Republic. Each of us are contributing to the re-establishment of our great race, and soon--the return of our glorious leader." Each of the interns gave a Hitler salute and wheeled the deceased out of the dorm. It took four trips apiece to transport each female from the dorm to the awaiting basement oven.

As the last three bodies were removed, Hausser placed his arms over his head and gave himself a long stretch. "Tomorrow morning when they ask about the other girls, tell them they have been transferred to an off-island facility and will return in a few weeks. That should satisfy them. With us now in possession of our Fuhrer's DNA from the stolen Moscow items, and our final ten female subjects, we will conclude our groundbreaking experiment--assuming none of them become rejects. Until then, I must get some rest. Gute Nacht."

"Gute Nacht," Herr Doctor.

Having left her house in Newark an hour earlier than normal to get a good jump on preparing her budget report due the following Friday, Jeannie beat Ismail to the FBI bureau office in San Francisco. That was one aspects of her Assistant Special Agent in Charge job she hated, that and having to handle occasional agent complaints. She had been successful in flying under the radar in regard to all the corruption and politics being revealed in the top FBI echelon. The director had recently been terminated by the president, but she was aware corruption ran a lot deeper. She just wanted to be the best agent she could be and hoped to avoid having to take sides. That, according to her SAC (Special Agent in Charge) Lomax, would be a career stopper. Retirement was looking better every day.

But retirement currently was not in the cards. First, she loved her job; and secondly, she had not yet reached retirement age. After retiring, her father became bored and returned to working part-time. Sharing many of her father's personality characteristics, she realized she either had to find a hobby to occupy her time after retirement or continue working.

Fortunately, the San Francisco Bay Area was ripe with crime and she and her team were kept busy. There was little time for gossiping and complaining about higher ups that could quickly lead to trouble. She was extremely proud of her team and their recent major investigation successes. Both she and Ismail had been decorated by the president for their work in stopping a group of jihadists from blowing up the BART (Bay Area Rapid Transit) tube leading from San Francisco to Oakland, and they had recently solved two serial killer cases and a huge Indian casino armored car robbery as well.

Those were the days, she thought as she completed the budgeting paperwork for the next fiscal year using the latest ZBB (Zero Based Budgeting). As a manager, she was required to build a budget from the ground up, starting from zero. Once popular in the 1970s, interest in ZBB had diminished over the past few decades due to the large amount of paperwork and data that had to be managed after ZBB was put into practice. However, thanks to the availability of cloud-based budgeting software and the growing popularity of performance management in business, Zero-Based Budgeting was experiencing a comeback and the FBI adopted it once again.

She recalled telling SAC Lomax the year before that she thought the bean counters of the Bureau should gather in D.C. after returning from their respective Ivy League universities where many picked up their left-wing Marxist ideologies and come up with a new and workable accounting method, instead of complicated add-on procedures to justify their positions. Not to her surprise, Lomax agreed, but said it had to be done.

So, for the past three years Jeannie grudgingly started the ZZB process, but did it in a half-hearted manner, knowing that Lomax was more number oriented than she could force herself to be and would make her work look presentable. "Hey boss. I see you're hard at it, huh?" Ismail commented as he placed a hot cup of coffee on Jeannie's desk.

"God, I hate this shit," she responded without saying thank you. "Damn it! Why do we have to do this each year? Why can't those assholes in Washington just add 10% across the board and be done with it."

"Hey," Ismail said. "That's why you make the big bucks."

"Screw you, buddy!" she said smiling.

She and Ismail had been together for a long time. They worked at the same field office across the bay in Roseville when it was attacked by an urban terrorist group known as the Sons and Daughters of Liberty. Their leader, who Jeannie simply called Joey, was responsible for the death of her fiancé, Ricky Pinheiro, an NSA agent and Ismail's cousin. When Jeannie accepted the Assistant Special Agent in Charge position in San Francisco, she requested Ismail's transfer as well as her two top IT experts, Darcy and Burk.

"So, besides stopping by to harass me, is there anything else going on I need to know about?" Jeannie asked.

"Nothing really. The SAC volunteered us to help track down the labs expecting the spiders. I was hoping that maybe some other agency would take the investigation over. You know how excited I was when he told me. We've also been requested by the San Mateo Sheriff's Department to assist in an apparent abduction. It's about three weeks old already, so good luck with that," Ismail replied.

"Why did they wait so long to ask for our assistance?" Jeannie asked.

"Initially they thought the victim left of her own volition. She had a fight with her boyfriend at a political rally in the city, one of those Black Lives Matter protests. They began fighting when she questioned the real motivation behind the group. One thing led to another, and she told him she was through and left. They lived in an apartment in San Mateo. Both work at one of the high-tech firms in Santa Clara, and the boyfriend thought she would show up for work the next day, but she didn't. After contacting relatives and friends to discover her whereabouts for two days with no success, he contacted the police. They played around with it and got nowhere, so now they're trying to throw it all on us."

"Sounds about right. I'd love to work it with you, but I have all this shit to do," she said, smacking her right hand on the pile of paperwork in front of her.

"Problem?" asked SAC Lomax who entered the room and stood behind Ismail. A little embarrassed, Jeannie laughed and said in a sarcastic tone, "No, sir. Not a problem at all. I love doing this necessary paperwork while my team is chasing bad guys."

"Well, I may have something to take you away from all this paperwork. I received a call from an Agent Delaney of Interpol. I think you know him."

"Sure," Jeannie said. "His agency helped us in the Ark of the Covenant investigation. Remember, Frank Silva and his Banshees?"

"Oh yeah! Now I know why his name rang a bell," Lomax continued. "Anyway, he'd like to meet with you two about a sex trafficking case Interpol is working on. Why don't you give me what you have of your ZBB so far and I'll handle it. I mean, since it's so necessary."

"Thank you, boss," Jeannie said, grabbing her jacket off the back of the chair, and with Ismail, beginning the walk to the parking garage.

NINE

Interpol (International Criminal Police Organization) had a small office located near the financial district in San Francisco. The organization consists of 194 member countries and was established to help police in all countries work together to make the world a safer place. To accomplish this, Interpol enables countries to both share and access criminal data and offers a range of technical and operational support. Its databases not only have information on crimes and criminals (from names and fingerprints to stolen passports), they're accessible in real-time by all member countries.

Interpol is staffed by both police and civilians and has headquarters in Lyon, France, a global complex for innovation in Singapore, and several satellite offices in various regions of the world. Their expertise supports national efforts to combat the three most pressing types of criminal activity: terrorism, cybercrime, and organized crime. Officials working in investigative areas such as support, field operations, training, and networking operate a variety of activities alongside member countries.

Jeannie and Ismail first met Interpol Bureau Chief Sean Delaney while they were investigating the anticipated Ark of the Covenant theft. Decorated Afghanistan and Iraq war heroes, Frank Silva and his platoon nicknamed "Banshees," used their military expertise to further their criminal activities. Silva had met a biblical historian/professor, Dr. Nancy Bell, who believed she knew the location of the holy relic--the actual Ark of the Covenant containing the remains of the Ten-Commandments. Since the Ark was believed to be located in Ethiopia, well outside the jurisdiction of the FBI, Jeannie reached out to Interpol, and thus met Delaney for the first time during that interaction.

When they entered the Interpol office, they saw Agent Delaney looking over the shoulder of a relatively new receptionist whom they had met earlier during their last visit. "Agent Loomis, Agent Flores, nice to see you again," Delaney said.

"You have a good memory. It's been several years," Ismail said.

"Yes, and we don't want to talk about that particular case, do we?" Delaney commented while motioning them to his office. "How could anyone forget the names of two of the FBI's finest?" Delaney said as he walked around the desk to his chair. Without waiting for an invite, Jeannie and Ismail sat down on two chairs opposite the desk. "I have to admit, you two have been involved in some very successful investigations. I hope your karma will brush off on me."

"Thank you," Jeannie said. "Our SAC told us you were investigating a sex-trafficking ring." Jeannie noticed that Delaney had not seemed to age since they last met when she flew to Ethiopia on her own dime to reinvestigate the Ark of the Covenant case, an experience she had not shared with others, not even Ismail. At the time she felt she had all bases covered in their investigation, but what puzzled her was the disappearance of Frank Silva and the Banshees, as well as Dr. Bell and the yacht that might have contained the Ark if it had been successfully stolen. When she arrived, she found that the chapel--supposedly containing the Ark and under the security of a lone monk--seemed to be undisturbed. There was no evidence of a break in, nor did any of the towns' people talk about an incident occurring at the chapel. For Jeannie, it was essentially a worthless trip.

She estimated Delaney to be about 6'1" with an athletic build. He had dark brown hair with a sprinkle of gray--styled like that of Sean Connery, the original James Bond. His hazel eyes were one of his best features, she thought, and of course, she loved his British accent. Every time she had seen him, he was immaculately dressed. She suspected he was wearing an Armani charcoal gray suit or some other designer brand, but definitely not an off-the-rack suit. His look was complete with a purple silk shirt and coordinated tie.

"Yes, right. So, Agent Loomis and Agent Flores," he began before being interrupted by Jeannie.

"Please, Agent Delaney. Call me Jeannie," and pointing to her partner, "Ismail."

"Splendid. With that in mind, my first name is Sean.

"Like Sean Connery?" Ismail asked, trying to suppress a laugh. Jeannie hit him on his right shoulder.

"Sorry Sean. I can't take him anywhere."

"Oh, precisely. Yes, Sean like double-0-seven himself, I'm afraid." Smiling at Ismail, he reached for a thick office file that had been lying on the left corner of his desk. He opened it and spread out over thirty photos of women, all approximately the same age and all blonds.

"My God!" Jeannie said. "They all look alike."

"You suspect a serial?" Ismail asked Delaney while looking at the photos.

"Frankly we don't know. In fact, none of the law enforcement agencies of our associated countries have any concrete ideas. That is why, Jeannie, I hope you and your team can give it a shake and then give us your perspective. I know you have a history in the bureau as a behavioralist and that you have a doctorate in psychology," he said, looking at Jeannie, "And well, we are frankly grasping for straws."

Jeannie did not respond. She seemed to be lost in the sea of photographs now extending from one corner of Delaney's desk to the other. "Is there a restroom I could use?" Ismail politely asked.

"Certainly." Delaney opened his office door and pointed in the direction of the restrooms. He returned to his desk and sat, looking at Jeannie who seemed not to notice. Finally, she looked up.

"Oh, sorry," she said. "The similarities are striking. Serial killers have a type, you know. Body type, hair style and so on. But these individuals, as I said, could almost pass as identical twins, except there are so many of them. The most remarkable feature is their eyes. I've never heard of a serial killer making sure that in addition to body type, they all had the same eye color."

"May I ask you a question Jeannie, and I hope you don't take offense?" Delaney asked somewhat shyly after a pause.

"No, please," she responded.

"I'm wondering if there is a Mr. Loomis at home?"

Not expecting this question, Jeannie blushed and gave her normal response of saying no and waving her ring finger in the air. "Doesn't mean much now a days, but no ring on me means no husband at home. My fiancé, NSA agent Ricky Pinheiro, was killed a few years ago in a shootout with the remaining members of the Sons and Daughters of Liberty. I'm still not sure I'm over the shock to be honest. And you, Agent Delaney, I mean, Sean?"

Clearing his throat and caressing his tie, Delaney said no. He added that he had had a wife, but she died of pancreatic cancer several years ago and his job now pretty much takes up his free time.

"Sorry for your loss. I know what you mean," Jeannie said. "I have a cabin up in Idaho that I love, yet I'm rarely able to get up there."

"Perhaps in the near future, you might accept an invitation to dinner?" Delaney asked. Jeannie could feel a little stir in her chest like she got when she first met Ricky Pinheiro, her deceased fiancé.

"I'd like that," she said, as Ismail re-entered the room.

"So, what's the plan?" Ismail asked, looking at Jeannie for an answer. Jeannie turned from Ismail to Delaney and asked if she could get copies of the photos to take back to the bureau. He called his secretary and when she arrived, he asked her to copy the set.

"Would it be possible to get two sets?" Jeannie asked. "I'd like to take a set home as well." "Absolutely," Delaney said, as he handed the photos to his secretary who was looking at Ismail and smiling.

When the secretary returned with the original photos and copies, Delaney handed the photo set to Jeannie. Ismail and Jeannie stood to leave and shook hands with Delaney. "I'll call you once my team and I are able to do a little brainstorming," Jeannie said.

"Great, and thank you both for coming so quickly," he said, hoping to convey that his feelings were directed more to Jeannie than Ismail.

When they got back to Ismail's bureau's Crown Vic, he looked at Jeannie. "Hey, did you notice? Delaney's secretary has the hots for me."

"Dream on! She obviously needs glasses," Jeannie said.

"No, honestly, when she gave Delaney copies of those photos, she locked eyes with me and gave me a seductive smile. I'm telling you. When you got it, you got it!"

"Still haven't seen anyone about your delusions of grandeur, have you?" Jeannie said, while still thinking about Sean.

TEN

After leaving the Interpol office, Jeannie and Ismail were both hungry, so they stopped at a nearby Panda Express for Chinese food. "Tell me, what are your plans involving Delaney?" Ismail asked, biting into a Spring Roll. "He's a handsome devil, isn't he?"

Jeannie caught herself blushing and tried to convince Ismail that it was a reaction to some Chinese hot mustard she had just eaten. There's no way he overheard the banter between me and Sean, was there? she asked herself. "You have to admit, all photos of those females were freaky. All about the same height, weight, and hair and eye color. Like I told him, I'm not aware of a serial killer selecting his victims so precisely--down to eye color. I want to set the photos up in our briefing room for the rest of the team, but I'll put that off until tomorrow. I need to sleep on it first. In the meantime, let's hit the lab addresses and finish the spider case."

"God, you had to bring up spiders while I'm eating lunch!" Ismail said with a hint of disgust.

The first stop was a building down the road from the University of California, Berkeley campus. From the outside it looked like a portion of a strip mall, but someone had placed UC decals on the front windows, setting it apart from the other buildings. Nothing indicated what department of the UC campus was housed there. They entered the building and were greeted by a green haired female around 22 years old with numerous piercings in her lip, nostrils, and eyebrows, and heavily tattooed. Patches of underarm hair protruded from her tank top, revealing she was braless.

"Cops are here!" she shouted without looking up from the receptionist desk. She finally glanced upward, waiting for either Jeannie or Ismail to state their purpose for being there. Jeannie pulled out her FBI badge and asked to speak to the manager.

"Scott. They want to see you. You're in deep shit now, buddy," she said, casting her eyes back to the magazine on the desk. Jeannie looked at Ismail who rolled his eyes.

A short male pushed one side of a swinging door open and approached the counter. "Can I help you?" he asked. Jeannie estimated that he was around the same age as the tattoo enthusiast but carried the weight of someone in charge of the establishment. He also sported tattoos--on both arms as well as the side of his neck. There were no piercings that either Jeannie or Ismail could see. Jeannie showed him her badge and asked if there was a place they could talk privately? He escorted them to an office to the side of the swinging doors, walked around to the far side of a metal desk and motioned for them to take a seat.

"What exactly do you do here?" Ismail asked.

"We're part of the main UC campus. We breed and house most of the lab animals used by the biology and medical departments. Is there a problem?"

"Exactly what type of animals do you house and breed here?" Jeannie asked.

"Agents, I can assure you we comply with all the strict regulations of the state and federal government, and the UC campus network."

"That's not what I asked you. Can you be more specific about the types of animals you have here?"

"Well, we have a lot of rats and mice, as you might expect. We also house and care for monkeys that are used by our Psychology Department for psychological experiments, but they're not mistreated in any way. At one time we had numerous aquariums when we had our Marine Biology Department here in Berkeley, but that changed when the UC campuses at Santa Cruz, Santa Barbara and San Diego each developed their own programs. Humboldt State, although not part of the UC system, has an excellent Marine Biology program also, and they took some of the aquariums and fish."

"Have you ever seen this man?" Ismail asked, placing a picture of the Australian Melcum Williams on the desk with the picture facing Scott. Scott's face turned bright red, and he began perspiring under the nose. He picked up the photo, acting like he was really giving it a once over, then placed it back on the table, denying any knowledge of the Australian.

"Beside lab rats and other animals you say you have here, how many spiders do you keep?" Jeannie asked.

Scott retracted his hand from the top of the metal desk where he was resting it, leaving sweat marks behind. Seeing that, he tried to nonchalantly wipe it up. "Spiders? We don't keep arachnids here."

"Where do you keep them?" Ismail asked, thinking he and Jeannie had Scotty-boy on the ropes.

"No. I mean, we never have kept spiders here. Sometimes we have a few harmless snakes, but never spiders."

Not letting up, Jeannie asked for a tour of the establishment. Surprisingly, Scott leaped out of his chair at the request and motioned for them to follow. Jeannie recalled what Dr. Stronberg had said about illicit trafficking of spiders being "off the books," and with Scott using the facility tour to contain his guilt, Jeannie knew they would find nothing. Sure enough, and to Ismail's relief, they failed to see a single arachnid.

Walking back to their vehicle, Jeannie asked Ismail to drop her off at the bureau so she could start a workup of the sex-trafficking case for Delaney, and to follow-up on the last two labs. "If you need to take someone with you, you big baby, go ahead. You'll probably get stonewalled just like old Scotty-boy just did, but we can say we followed up and CYA (covered our asses)." Surmising he would not have to see spiders, Ismail agreed.

"What a man!" Jeannie said. "Better yet, let's both go to the bureau, and you can contact San Mateo about their missing female case. If you think it's necessary, go ahead and drive down there to see what they have and what avenues they've explored. I think the spider case can wait. No sense driving back up here afterward, so when you're finished, head home and harass your darling wife."

"Sounds good to me."

Back at his desk, Flores called the San Mateo Sheriff's Department. After going through the normal bureaucratic process to locate the correct investigator, he learned that the lead detective handling the case was a Sgt. Tom Baldwin.

"Sgt. Baldwin, this is Agent Ismail Flores with the San Francisco FBI. I'm calling about your missing person case--the female from three weeks ago. Any new information?"

"I'm afraid not, and naturally her parents are putting heat on the department. She was their only child."

"Look, depending on your schedule, I was hoping to drive down there and look at your investigation to date, if that works for you. You know, fresh eyes and all."

"Hey, that would be great. We can at least let the parents know we've reached out to the FBI. What time do you think you'll arrive?"

ELEVEN

Due to a traffic accident that had happened earlier, Ismail's normal 45-minute drive to the San Mateo Sheriff's Department took an extra 20 minutes. He caught himself smiling at the thought of his justification for driving down the Bayshore freeway to the Sheriff's Department. It was simply to avoid working on the boring spider case. He knew Jeannie suspected that would happen and the reason she suggested it.

Sgt. Baldwin was a male of average build, sporting the beginning of male pattern baldness he tried to disguise with a combover. Ismail had given up on that years ago, and with a small amount of hair on the sides, he often thought of just going for the Michael Jordan look and be done with it. After greetings and handshakes, Baldwin escorted Ismail though the sheriff's office to the Missing Person's Bureau. Instead of meeting at his desk, he took Ismail to a small interview room where he had everything of interest on display.

A wall was covered with photos of who Ismail presumed was the missing female, including pictures of her home, family members, friends, and a picture of what looked like a nightclub. Nearing the display board, he noticed that she had all the characteristics of photos he saw at the Interpol office. She was blonde, the approximate same height and weight as the others--and had mesmerizing eyes. "Damn!" he said out loud.

"Got something?" Baldwin asked.

"Maybe. Tell me about the case," Ismail requested.

"Her name is Judy Christianson, twenty-three years old, and born and raised in Foster City. She has a sister and a brother, but she's the oldest. She attends college and is an A-student and wants to be a medical doctor. According to her parents, on Friday night three weeks ago, she and this lady, Cindy Hartman, went clubbing at this place (pointing at a picture). It's a bistro that turns into a nightclub at night, targeting Judy's age group. According to Cindy, they ordered drinks at the bar and then mingled with the crowd. About 45-minutes later, Cindy couldn't locate Judy and checked the bathroom to see if she were there. Not finding her, she walked through the club, thinking that maybe she somehow missed her. Beginning to panic, she contacted the manager who made an announcement over the PA system, requesting that Judy meet her friend at the manager's office."

"She never showed?" Ismail asked.

"No. No one's seen her since."

Ismail had a plan to get started. "Look, we're currently working on a case with Interpol that involves females who have disappear in several countries after visiting bars and nightclubs. Most have occurred in Western Europe. When I saw Judy's photo, her appearance was strikingly similar to that of the other missing women, and the M.O. (modus operandi) appears to be the same. Victims go into a bar, order a drink, become disoriented and walk outside for fresh air, then disappear. Families don't receive ransom demands and no bodies have been found. If you can give me copies of what you have, especially Judy's photos, I'll take them back to my supervisor and perhaps we can take the case off your hands."

"Fine with me. At least I can face her family and tell them we've turned the case over to you guys."

Having received copies of the entire case file, Ismail returned to his vehicle and called Jeannie. She answered with, "Don't tell me you found more spiders!"

"No, and not if I can help it. Hey, I'm leaving the San Mateo Sheriff's Department and guess what? I think that whoever's responsible for abducting those females Interpol is working on, struck down here as well."

"Oh shit! Blonde hair, blue eyes?" Jeannie asked.

"Boss, she could be their twins. Same M.O. Disappeared from a nightclub after getting a drink. Missing for about 45 minutes to an hour. Friend searches the place, panics and the victim is missing. Police go to check with the bartender, and he's also vanished. I have their entire case file and I'll bring it in tomorrow morning, but you might want to call James Bond and let him know."

There was no immediate response from Jeannie, not because of the James Bond reference, but because she was becoming aware of the case's increasing enormity. "Okay, look. I'm going to call Delaney now and fill him in. No need for you to come back here today. I'll ask him to come to the bureau tomorrow with everything he has. I think it's time to bring the whole team together and decide how to proceed. See you in the morning."

The next day before Jeannie arrived at the bureau, Ismail took Burk to visit the last two labs on their list. Burk had survived the shootout at the Roseville field office where they had both been assigned with Jeannie as their IT specialist. It was here that she was seriously wounded and subsequently lost her fetus.

"Thanks for asking me to come along. It's nice to get out of the computer lab occasionally. So, who are we going after?" Burk asked. Ismail filled him in while driving to the lab located in the industrial area near the Oakland estuary.

"The Australian gave us his contact at this lab. Some guy named Ronald," Ismail said. "He arranges to meet Ronald at a fast-food restaurant where he delivers the spiders for cash. What Ronald does with them, he had no idea. I'm hoping that by simply dropping in unannounced, we can catch him with the evidence we need to prosecute. We shall see. Here we are."

The lab was housed in a former corner grocery store. Ismail remembered the building's familiarity from when he was a kid, getting a dollar from his grandmother and walking to her corner store to buy as much candy and gum he could get for a buck. A bell was activated when they entered the building, just like it did when it was his grandma's store. "Can I help you?" an Asian woman seated at a small desk in the corner asked.

"Yes. I'm Special Agent Flores and this is Special agent Burk. We're with the FBI. Can we speak with Ronald?"

"He's not here now. I expect him back sometime this afternoon. Can I help?"

"What type of business do you run here?" Ismail asked.

"We milk wasps for their venom," she replied matter-of-factly. Lost for words, neither Burk nor Ismail said anything. "Right now, we're kind of slow since it's winter-time. But during the summer months when wasps seem to be everywhere, we're very busy. When people's picnics or backyard BBQs are disrupted by wasps and bees, they call their local exterminators. When the exterminators arrive, they remove the hives and occupants and freeze them. Then they sell the wasps and bees to us, and we remove their venom sacks. We in turn sell them to labs who make the actual antivenom for stings. I can give you a tour if you want."

"Where do you keep the spiders?" Burk asked.

"Spiders! Hell, we don't keep them here. I mean, I know Ronald used to work with spiders a long time ago, but not here. No way! I hate spiders."

"Out of curiosity, how did Ronald work with spiders?" Burk inquired.

"First, they have to be alive, they're not like wasps or bees. You get them agitated, and then by using a little nose drop-like mechanism, you suck up the venom from their fangs. Fortunately, it doesn't take much of their venom to create an antivenom since their poison is a lot stronger than what we can get from wasps."

"So, when did you say Ronald will be back?" Ismail asked.

"Probably around three this afternoon, maybe earlier." Ismail handed her his business card and requested that Ronald call when he returned.

Knowing that Ismail intensely hatred spiders, Burk could not resist telling him there was a job awaiting him when he retires from the bureau--sucking venom from spiders. Ismail did not reply, but his stare conveyed his thoughts.

Once back in their car, Ismail called Jeannie. "Any luck?" she said upon answering the phone.

"No. A worker said they don't handle spiders, and judging from the way she spoke, I suspect she hates them as much as I do. Ronald, the name given as the buyer from our Australian smuggler, wasn't in, so I left a business card. We'll see if he calls back. We're heading to the last lab. How goes it there?"

"Frankly, I don't know if I'm making any progress at all. I posted all the photos in our briefing room with Darcey's help. She's running what info Delaney gave us on the victims through all data banks, but I think we'll only get the same information Interpol learned. I don't know if this is the work of one or two serial killers, or if it's an elaborate organized sex trafficking operation. I'm coming down with a damn headache, so I'm thinking about getting out of here early and brainstorm at home. Let me know if you get anything from the last lab."

TWELVE

"So far, this is the only place that looks like a lab," Ismail said, not expecting a reply from Burk. The lab was located in a single building painted bright white with blue trim, resembling a medical facility with manicured lawn and trimmed hedges, several trimmed in the traditional Niwaki style. A crystal clear pond with a waterfall located near the front door contained small koi swimming among floating water hyacinths. "Jeannie would love this," Ismail said.

The front door was locked, but a sign showed where the buzzer was located. Burk pushed it and the door was released by someone inside. Upon entering, the unmistaken smell of various pet foods, sawdust, and loud caws from several Macaws perched on a madrone branch made them feel as though they had entered a pet shop. A large bouncing Scarlet Macaw said "hello."

An older man came from the back of the store and greeted them. "Hello gentlemen. What can I do for you?"

This time Burk displayed his FBI badge and asked to speak with Tommy. "Sure, one minute," the man replied as he retreated to somewhere in the back.

Tommy was a white male in his forties, his head completely devoid of hair--obviously done by choice—that reflected the store's overhead lights. "FBI. Wow, this is a first. What can I do for you?" he asked.

"Are you the owner of this firm?" Ismail asked, already knowing from his interview with the Australian that he wasn't.

"No, that would be my dad. He was the person you just talked to. Do you want me to get him back?"

"No, that's alright. It's actually you we want to talk to," Ismail said, taking out the spider smuggler's photo. "Do you know this person?"

"Gee. He looks familiar. Could be a customer. I can't be sure. What did he do?"

Instead of answering Tommy's question, Ismail asked what type of business he was running.

"Well, as you can see, we specialize in exotic pets. Birds to be more precise. We don't import them. Instead, we take them off the hands of owners who, for whatever reason, can't care for them anymore. Many have picked up bad habits in their prior environment or have a disease that's got to be treated. This hyacinth macaw here is Pedro. As you can see, he's a feather picker. Tommy pulled a biscuit out of his shirt pocket and gave it to the parrot who took it in his beak and bounced up and down. This isn't caused by a disease, but by an owner who had a temper problem. When the owner got upset, he'd throw things around the room. Although the assaults weren't directed toward

Pedro, the bird became neurotic and started pulling out his feathers."

"So, what do you do with them after you treat them?" Burk asked.

"When we feel they're ready to re-enter someone's home, we list them for adoption on various websites, but a potential owner must go through a background check before we allow any of our birds to be taken. You know, do they have children at home? Are there other animals? Do they smoke? Have they ever had exotic birds before, and so on? What type of cage and environment the bird will live in."

"What about spiders?" Ismail asked.

Tommy instantly broke eye contact with both agents. He walked up to Pedro who had finished eating the treat and began stroking his chest. "Spiders? What do you mean?"

"I mean poisonous spiders. You know, like Sydney Funnel Web Spiders." Buying for time, Tommy bent down and picked up some of Pedro's feathers and gave the bird a short lecture about being a bad boy. "I'm sorry agents. As you can see, we only deal with exotic birds. I don't know why anyone would want a poisonous spider as a pet." His whole response came without re-establishing eye contact.

"Would it be okay if we had a look around? Burk asked.

"Sure. Please. Follow me." With that Tommy showed them the entire showroom, providing short stories about several of the parrots, and he reintroduced his father. No spiders were seen during the entire tour.

"Look Tommy. I'm going to level with you," Ismail said. "Your name was given to us by an individual under arrest for the illegal transportation of poison spiders that he said you were going to buy."

"No way man," Tommy responded. "He must have me confused with someone else. We only work with exotic birds, Macaws, Cockatoos, birds like that."

"So why would he implicate you?" Burk asked.

"I don't know. I honestly don't know."

"Tell you what Tommy, I'm not sure where this case is going to go, but if you or anyone you know is involved in this, you or they'd better think about getting an attorney." With that, Ismail and Burk turned and left.

"What do you think?" Ismail asked as they put on their seatbelts.

"He's lying through his teeth," Burk responded.

"Yep, but we don't have anything concrete to legitimately go after him. It's simply one person accusing another, and in this politically correct state, you would be hard pressed to find a DA who would prosecute with what we have."

THIRTEEN

Jeannie left the bureau a little before noon. The Ibuprofen she took before the drive seemed to help her headache. There was little commute traffic on her way home that hour of the day. She decided to take Highway 101 south to the Dumbarton Bridge instead of the Bay Bridge; there was always a 50/50 chance that an accident would occur on the Bay Bridge, or some road construction would reduce the number of lanes available--and there she would be, inhaling exhaust fumes from the other stranded travelers.

She passed the famous Painted Ladies of San Francisco and headed toward South San Francisco, passing the SFO and Cow Palace exits. In the past, she used to strain her head while going south on the freeway to get a view of Candlestick Park. She and her dad attended many 49ers and Giants games there. Good times. Now the entire park was gone; it had been razed to the ground.

The City-By-The-Bay politicians had plans to develop a large shopping mall there as well as housing units, but as usual nothing had been started, much less completed—all at a tremendous cost in tax money. No, Jeannie thought, the city that once was, is no more. The homeless and drug addicts congregate on the streets as no one enforces panhandling laws anymore. So much for a democrat-controlled city and state.

She made it home to Newark more quickly than normal and called ahead to the local Chick-fil-A on her cell, ordering a grilled chicken sandwich, fries and diet coke for pick-up. She liked the grilled chicken since she could get it in a wheat burrito wrap. Anything to justify the high carb, high calorie entrée for this evening, she thought to herself.

Having picked up her supper, she parked her bureau car in the driveway and opened the garage door. Her Red Corvette was parked inside, a vanity ride she felt she earned by properly saving and investing part of her salary. She quickly closed the garage door and entered her kitchen. "Alright! I made it inside my house without Delores catching me," she said out loud with a smile, and placed her food on the table.

Grabbing a dish, she took the bag of food to the dining table so she could check on her koi. Pulling a stool out from underneath the aquarium stand she opened a jar of food pellets she kept there and dropped pellets into their tank. "Hello guys, did you miss me? Boy, you guys are as hungry as I am." She watched for a few minutes to make sure they were all alright and free of disease or stress symptoms.

Back in the kitchen, she washed and dried her hands, grabbing her handgun, and returned to the dining room. Having placed the Glock on the seat next to her, she dug into the paper bag and removed the fries and sandwich, then returned to the kitchen and got a soft drink and her briefcase containing the missing women's photos she got from Delaney' secretary. Returning to the dining room, she laid the photos out on the table in no particular order and unwrapped her sandwich while stuffing a catsup drenched fry into her mouth.

The victim's name and birth date had been written on the back of each photo. After rapidly viewing the images, she turned them over and saw that each were between 21-25 years old. Not a one was younger or older. "Huh," she said out loud, looking at her koi. "Does that seem strange to you guys also? I mean, they almost all look identical. Blonde, five foot two, to five feet four. All with piercing blue eyes, and their ages are all in the same ballpark." Unlike talking things over with Ismail, her fish never offered feedback. According to Ismail, the female missing in San Mateo County should match these, she thought.

She finished her lunch and took the dirty dish and wrappings to the kitchen. Finishing her drink, she picked up the photos and wiped off the dining table. Addressing the fish tank she said, "Well, thanks you guys. You weren't much help, but I love you anyway," and gave them some extra food. That's when her doorbell rang. She thought it had to be Delores, and she was right.

Delores was her next-door neighbor and the neighborhood busybody and gossiper. She was also the captain of the neighborhood-alert program, a position she took very seriously. Nothing happened in the neighborhood that missed her observation. She had taken over the leadership role after a former board members objected to residents displaying Christmas lights and displays on their property. That was enough for Delores who not only took them on, but was elected as the new leader. She made it very uncomfortable for former board members, and her battles forced some to move. She and husband Walter had lived next door to Jeannie for several years. They were trustworthy, reliable, and super quiet at night. That aside, Delores did unknowingly help solve two of Jeannie's serial killer cases.

In one case, the Koufax serial murderer investigation, Jeannie and the Marin County Sheriff's department were frustrated at not being able to capture a killer who made no attempt to conceal his identity. Not only did he leave fingerprints at the scene of his crimes, he signed motel registration cards as well as allowing himself to be photographed. He played what Jeannie called the "Time Game," always a few minutes ahead of the responding police.

After discussing the Time Game case with Delores, Delores told Jeannie that it sounded like a movie she and her husband had just watched called the Highwaymen. In the film, two retired Texas Rangers were attempting to capture the infamous Bonnie and Clyde gang. Delores told Jeannie that they went around in circles, similar to what Jeannie and her team were experiencing, until they realized that Bonnie and Clyde always came back to their familiar haunts. That allowed them to set up an ambush and kill the two bank robbers. This story inspired Jeannie, and she and her team began focusing on Koufax's friends, relatives, and associates. Sure enough, he returned to his old haunts and was killed.

In another instance while Delores was still glowing from Jeannie's accolades in helping capture Koufax, Jeannie discussed another serial killer case she was working on with the San Jose Police Department. In that particular investigation, the suspect dismembered the bodies of elderly victims after killing them. All victims lived on orchards in rural Santa Clara County. Delores said that when she was a kid, she would go with her parents and siblings to her aunt and uncle's orchard and pick apricots. Sometimes she was scared because of the extra help brought in to assist when there was an excessive amount of fruit to be picked before spoilage. Delores's simple reference to extra farm personnel led to the killer's identification.

"Hi, Delores. How are you?" she asked, opening the front door.

"Oh, hi Jeannie. I'm fine. How are you? You sure are home early today."

"Yes, I have a headache and decided to come home and relax."

Delores unfolded a piece of heavy paper which Jeannie immediately recognized as a paper target used by most law enforcement agencies to qualify with their service weapons. This particular target showed a white bald male sporting a goatee in a crouched position, pointing a handgun at the viewer. Delores handed it to Jeannie.

"What's this?" Jeannie asked.

Grinning from ear to ear, Delores stood back as Jeannie started counting all the holes, starting in the 7-ring and progressing to the X ring which was dead center. One hit the paper suspect in the groin. "Wow! You shot this?" Jeannie asked.

"Yep. I even beat Walter, and he was in the military, you know."

"Delores! What have you been doing with your spare time? I can tell you haven't been baking."

"Well, with all of the riots taking place in Portland, Chicago, Seattle, and Los Angeles, you know those Antifa people, Walter and I decided that we needed to be better prepared if it spreads here in Newark. We signed up at a gun range that offered classes to seniors, and well, I guess I'm a natural."

"I would say you are! Damn girl, maybe you should become an FBI agent. I only see one shot hitting the suspect in the groin. Or was that done on purpose?"

"Oh, gosh. I'm too old for that," she said while checking her hair. For once she did not have curlers, so Jeannie surmised it must be an automatic response. "Yes, the shot in his private parts was intentional. I mean, if some pervert broke into my house, I don't want him to have his way with me."

"Well, that shot would definitely take care of his lust," replied Jeannie, thinking of her deceased fiancé up there in heaven rolling over with laughter.

"I know you're probably busy, so I'll get back home to Walter. Are you working any cases that might need some input?"

"Actually, things right now are a little slow. But don't you worry. You're two-for-two girl in solving cases for us, so if we run into a roadblock, I'll seek you out."

"Okay. Just let me know. Always glad to help the men and women in blue."

FOURTEEN

Jeannie took a hot shower and noticed that her headache was almost gone. She could not stop smiling, thinking about her visit with Delores. I'd hate to be a burglar breaking into her house, she thought to herself. Having dried off and putting on her thermal pants and Thin Blue Line t-shirt, she walked into her spare bedroom where she had laid the photos on her desk. She hung each picture on the wall, this time based on the date of disappearance.

She sat at her desk and pulled out a yellow legal pad. Opening to a fresh sheet, she drew a line down the center. On the left she wrote commonalities, and on the right, she wrote dissimilarities. Within a few minutes she finished and examined her work.

Commonalities	**Dissimilarities**
Age group: 21- 25	
Blonde hair:	Hair length and style
Piercing blue eyes	
5'2 – 5'4"	
Athletic figures	
Abducted	Different locations and times
Most taken from bar--drugged	Few taken from other locations

Jeannie thought she must be missing something. It had to be right in front of her, but she could not see it. There had to be a missing piece that would bring it all together, she believed. It always seemed to be the little things that help catch a suspect. Oh well, I'm not going to lose sleep over it, she thought to herself. Maybe her team's upcoming brainstorming session scheduled for the next day would come up with something. She heard her cell phone ring and remembered she had left it downstairs. Scurrying down the stairs she grabbed it in time but did not recognize the number. "Loomis," she said.

"Jeannie. This is Sean. Sean Delaney. I hope I'm not disturbing you."

"Not at all. I hope you got the message I left with your receptionist that we may have a similar abduction here in Foster City. She fits the profile. I have to tell you, I can't find a consistent thread yet, but my team and I will be starting on it in earnest tomorrow."

"I'm glad to hear that. I'm afraid that we too are coming up empty handed, but that's not why I called." He cleared his throat. "I was wondering if you might be free for dinner sometime this week?"

Jeannie's heart began to race. "I would love it," she said. "Do you have a date already circled?"

"Oh, no. I know your work schedule is probably worse than mine. I'm free any night, including tomorrow evening, unless that's too soon?"

"I don't know about having a worse schedule than yours. Tomorrow night would be great. Where would you like to meet?"

"Well, I thought we could go to a Fish and Chip restaurant down the street from here." He paused. "No, I am just joking," he said, trying to suppress a laugh.

"Actually, there's a Fish and Chip place very close to me that I go to maybe twice a month," Jeannie said.

"What I'm thinking is perhaps tomorrow evening, since we're both here in the city we could meet at Park Tavern on Stockton Street. Do you know where it is?"

"I'm sure I can find it. What time would you like to meet?"

"Oh, I'm quite open regarding time. What works for you and the FBI?" he asked in his flirtatious British accent.

"Well, I can meet you there at, say five p.m. How does that sound?"

"Splendid. I'm so looking forward to seeing you then. If something comes up, however, please call me. I'll understand. Have a nice rest of your evening, Jeannie."

"Wait, Sean. Are you still there?"

"Yes, I'm here."

"I was just thinking that since we'll be going out to dinner tomorrow night, if you have an opening in your schedule tomorrow, perhaps you could make a presentation to my team here at the bureau. I mean, you know this case much better than Ismail and I do, and you can handle questions from my team about the case. You know, what avenues you have already considered and so on. We can also review the San Mateo case. What do you think?"

"I think it's an excellent idea. What time shall I be there?"

By the time Jeannie finished her phone call with Delaney, she found herself in front of her aquarium. She climbed on her stool and opened the hood of the tank, dropping food pellets into her koi's awaiting mouths. "Hey guys, guess who's going out to dinner with 007 tomorrow night?"

FIFTEEN

Angelika Hartmann arrived at the Call Me Drella Club in Munich with her girlfriend, Ingrid. They tipped the cab driver, stepped out of the vehicle and rearranged their party dresses before entering the club. Call Me Drella was one of the most exhilarating night clubs, in not just Germany, but the world. The club's name was a symbiosis of two fairy tale characters, Dracula and Cinderella. As the story goes, by day Dracula was shy, slept, and avoided sunlight. As night fell, however, the glamorous princess awakened in him and he searched for blood to quench his thirst.

Both women liked going there on Thursdays since the musical fare was from the 90s to present. Coming from wealthy families, the exorbitant costs of food and drink was not a problem. They also appreciated the club employees' costumes. A strict dress code allowed Angelika and Ingrid to dress to the tens. "You look hot girl," Ingrid said, watching Angelika adjust her red form-fitting sleeveless dress that stopped four inches above her knee and emphasized her cleavage, as well as the red, strappy heels.

It was a warm night, so there was no need to wear a jacket. "Let's party," came the reply. Neither noticed a dark sedan containing three men pulling to the curb as the two approached the club's entrance. The person in the passenger seat pulled out his cell phone and pressed a pre-set phone number. A few rings later, a male answered the phone. "Drella Club, can I help you?"

"The girl will be entering the club in a few seconds. She has blonde hair and is wearing a red short dress. She has a friend with her wearing a black dress. The friend is not the target. You know what to do once she places a drink order. We will be coming inside soon."

The place was jumping. The music was so loud that to speak with one another, the person talking had to place their lips next to the other's ear. "Let's get a drink and check out the crowd," Ingrid said. At the bar, a bartender said "Hi" and asked for their orders. As they waited, they turned to watch the crowd of gyrating bodies dancing to You Can't Touch This by MC Hammer.

"Here you go ladies. Do you want to open a tab?" the bartender asked. Ingrid said they would and the two walked toward an empty table near the dance floor, swaying back and forth to the beat of the music and trying not to spill their drinks. Two of the three men waiting in the sedan entered the club and approached the bar. The same bartender that served Angelika and Ingrid met them and nodded in the direction of the two women. Both men order a beer and watched as their target got up with Ingrid and began to dance to the next song, Krypnonite by Three Doors Down.

A few minutes later, Angelika motioned to Ingrid who had accepted a guy's dance invitation that she was going to the bathroom. The men saw she was already unsteady on her feet, and as she entered the bathrooms hallway they approached, grabbed each of her arms and acted as if they were helping. Instead, they led her to a waiting sedan outside. The awaiting driver opened the rear door and pushed Angelika onto the rear seat. One man climbed in behind her and the other returned to the passenger seat. A moment later the car took off.

Ingrid did not notice that Angelika was missing until almost 15 minutes later when she realized that Angelika had not returned from the restroom. Having searched the bathroom and the entire club, she asked a different individual working at the bar if he would make an announcement over the PA system for Angelika, which he did. There was no response. With that, the club's manager notified the police.

SIXTEEN

Jeannie assembled her team at 9:30 a.m. In addition to Burk and her IT specialist, Darcy, there were another ten agents. Ismail was the last to walk in, escorting Delaney. Jeannie's heart leaped a little when she saw Sean.

"Good morning, everyone," Jeannie said, walking to the front of the group. "We've been asked to assist Interpol in what they believe is a sex-trafficking ring operating both here in the U.S. and Western Europe." Darcy and Burk had already placed the missing women's pictures on the whiteboard. "As you can see, all of these young ladies are strikingly similar, down to their blue eyes. I want to introduce Agent Delaney from Interpol who will discuss their investigation, but before I do, I want everyone to know that yesterday Ismail learned of a similar kidnapping in our own backyard, Foster City. The suspect or suspects used the same method of abduction. If you'll hold your questions 'till the end, we'll put our collective heads together and brainstorm. Agent Delaney," Jeannie said, as she took a seat in the front row.

"Ladies and Gentlemen, I'd like to first congratulate you on the outstanding investigative work you've done over the years here at the San Francisco bureau. Your handling of the jihadist terrorist group and the Star Chamber case are still talked about today in our field offices. It's because of your proven abilities and expertise that I'm here today, reaching out to you for whatever support you can give Interpol in locating these missing women. Sadly, we have nothing."

Pointing his hand toward the photos, Delaney continued. "As you can see, these unfortunates all look like they're related. They're similar in looks, stature, and age, and yet to date we can't make any connection between them. None of them are physically related. They didn't work at the same place of employment, nor did they attend the same school. The abductions appear to be random, but well planned. Eleven women have been reported missing from the east coast here in America, mostly New York. Looks like we'll be adding the Foster City case to these, the first from the western part of the U.S. That brings the number of missing to twelve. The others were abducted in Western Europe, mostly Germany and Austria.

"To date, no ransom demands have been made, nor has anyone or group made claim of being responsible for the kidnappings. We have little physical evidence, and what we do have hasn't helped solve the case. I think that perhaps I should ask for questions now, and we'll see where that leads us."

Darcy was the first to raise her hand. "Is there a specific reason Interpol is treating this as a sex-trafficking investigation versus a very active serial killer or killers scenario?"

"As you know, Interpol is an international organization," Delaney said, as he began his answer. "The larger the organization, the more politics involved. It could very well be the act of one or more serial killers, but most police agencies in Europe, and even here in your country, don't want to admit that a possible serial killer is operating in their jurisdiction. Some of these kidnappings have taken place within days of each other. I'm not as qualified as Agent Loomis to address the psyche of a serial killer, but normally they don't act this quickly until they begin to expediate their kills. Whether it's the act of one or more serial killers, or even a cult, we frankly have no leads directing us where to go next. It does appear there are at least two to three individuals involved in the actual kidnappings."

Jeannie spoke up without raising her hand. "With those points in mind, I was thinking that if it were the work of one or more serial killers, why haven't bodies been found? If it were a cult, I can't believe they could have stayed off everyone's radar for so long. When was the first known abduction?"

Delaney looked at notes he pulled from his breast pocket. "The first known kidnapping occurred in 2005; approximately sixteen years ago."

"Sixteen years ago? Jesus!" Burk said, not expecting an answer.

Delaney continued, "If I recall correctly, your Green River Murderer killed his first victims in the early 1980s and wasn't captured until 2001. He was convicted on 49 counts of murder, but said he wasn't sure how many more there were. So, sadly, to go back to your question Darcy, it could be a very sophisticated and intelligent serial killer who has help, or groups of killers. As I stated, we do believe there's more than one person conducting the actual abductions, as they appear to be highly organized.

"Regarding cults, I think the sheer number of missing can rule that out. We could be wrong, but Interpol has no knowledge of any active cults operating between the U.S. and Western Europe. It could possibly be a satanic cult using these unfortunates as sacrifices. Again, I don't' feel that's the case."

Seeing no more raised hands, he continued. "Instead of going over each abduction, I'll just review a few since the method used is similar in all cases. I've brought our case files with me. They contain everything we have about each incident, and you can review them. Hopefully, Agent Loomis can get them duplicated so each of you will have your own set."

"Darcy...," Jeannie said, looking at her and indicating this would be her first job following the meeting. Darcy nodded.

"I'm on it," Darcy replied.

"In most cases, the victims attend a bar gathering, visit a nightclub or something similar. We believe they're given a drug in either their drink or food and become incapacitated. The kidnappers then quickly make an escape with their target. So, with that in mind, I suspect you have someone administering a drug and then following the victim outside where others are waiting."

"Sorry, Agent Delaney," Jeannie interrupted. "I assume that security cameras in the area have been reviewed?"

"Yes, in several cases. But by the time we traced the involved vehicles' license plate numbers, the cars were engulfed in flames, netting us nothing. Also, the photos were of such poor quality that we could only make out that the suspects were white males ranging in age from thirty to forty. The VINs always came back as stolen vehicles." He waited to see if Jeannie or anyone else had additional questions. Receiving none he went on.

"Only a few of the kidnappings took place in the dead of night where victims were taken from their homes or apartments. No evidence was found in their domiciles. Chloroform or perhaps a stun gun may have been used. We thought we might have our first break in a case when a female in Berlin, fitting the same description as these young ladies, broke free from her abductors. She was walking home from school when a van drove up next to her and a man jumped out of the passenger seat while the sliding door was opened by someone else. Before the second man who opened the sliding door could grasp her firmly, she kicked the first kidnapper in his, uh, in his private area and he released her." Jeannie thought it was cute that Delaney blushed and stumbled instead of stating the potential victim kicked the suspect in the balls.

"She ran screaming back to the school yard, but since she never looked back, she could only provide a limited amount of information about the vehicle. It was later found abandoned and gutted by fire. Both suspects were described as white and of average height and weight. It happened so quickly she didn't notice anything specific about the two assailants. Only the passenger spoke, yelling to the other kidnapper. He spoke in German with no distinct accent." No one asked any further questions.

"Alright everyone, let's take a break," Jeannie said. "We have bagels, donuts, coffee and tea on the back table. Ismail walked up to Delaney and asked him if he wanted a cup of coffee. "Tea would be nice," Delaney said. " I'll follow you to the table."

Jeannie walked with them. "See what I mean. We don't have much other than a lot of missing women. It's as if once the kidnapping happens, the victims vanish into thin air." Delaney left his comments hanging in the air between Ismail and Jeannie.

Jeannie looked at Ismail. "I know what you're going to say," she said.

Delaney looked at Ismail who said, "When we have a case like this, either Jeannie or I tell the other that all we need is one little piece, one break, to start solving the puzzle. Frankly, I think that's what's missing. One little piece of evidence or information that will solve this case."

"Yes," Delaney said. "But how many more young women will have to disappear before we get that missing piece?"

SEVENTEEN

The brainstorming session at the bureau produced little. However, everyone agreed the Foster City-San Mateo County case was so similar too the one at hand that it had to be included in the investigation. SAC Lomax would notify the Sheriff and inform him that the FBI would take over the case. Several theories were debated, but neither Jeannie nor Delaney felt the speculations were realistic. The two continued to scan the Interpol abduction files.

Ismail instructed two agents to begin a paper chase of the three labs to see if any monetary deposits were related to spider sales, making sure that SAC Lomax heard him give the order. Can't let the big guy think I'm not working the spider case, he thought to himself. He had already lost interest in the case and wanted to focus on the sex-trafficking or serial killer investigation.

Jeannie sent everyone home at 4:00 p.m., asking them to continue brainstorming on their own and to reconvene the next morning at 9:30. She was glad Ismail headed out the door before she and Delaney left together for their drive to the restaurant. Jeannie was amazed at how nervous she was once they left the bureau. The conversation during the drive covered points raised in the briefing. In between, Jeannie had random thoughts about the last time she went out to dinner with someone she was interested in, realizing her last date was with her murdered fiancé, Ricky Pinheiro.

The Park Tavern restaurant was located in the North Beach area of San Francisco adjacent to Chinatown, the Financial District, and Russian Hill. The neighborhood was known as San Francisco's "Little Italy" and has historically been home to a large Italian American population, largely from Northern Italy. It still has many Italian restaurants, although many other ethnic groups currently live in the vicinity. It was also the beatnik subculture's historic center and has since become one of San Francisco's main nightlife districts. As well, it was a residential neighborhood populated by a mix of young urban professionals, families, and Chinese immigrants.

Although Jeannie had never been to the restaurant, she had heard it was known for its classic American Tavern menu, great bar, signature cocktails and fabulous atmosphere. From its description, she could picture it in downtown London. Like most restaurants in the city, space was almost as valuable as its location. The interior had approximately twenty-five tables placed extremely close together. Fortunately, it was early for the dinner crowd and they were seated in a relatively secluded far corner with space to themselves.

"God, I sure hope they have Fish and Chips," Jeannie said, eyeing the menu handed to her while smiling and glancing at Sean.

"I'm afraid not. But they are known for their Chicken Milanese. We'll have to get Fish and Chips some other day." Jeannie blushed when Sean alluded to a second dinner date so early in the evening. They both chose the Milanese and shared a bottle of white wine.

"I have to tell you Sean, this is the first time I've gone out on a dinner date in a long time. This is really nice."

"Same for me. After my wife died several years ago, I seemed to dive into my work even more so. She developed pancreatic cancer, and chemo didn't help. We never had children, and with relatives living far away in Europe, I handled most of her care until she was put in hospice. Although I'm currently stationed here, the job requires a lot of international traffic. For a single person that might seem glamorous, and don't get me wrong, it was at first. But it put a tremendous amount of strain on our marriage before she got sick, as you can imagine." He stopped, lost in thought.

"I'm so sorry about your wife. Although Ricky and I were engaged, we had only been together for less than a year. Does the hurt of losing someone ever go away?"

"I'm afraid not. There always seems to be something that brings them back into your thoughts. I mean, at first I still felt her presence in our home. Even after giving her clothes to charities, I would always find something lying about that brought her back to me, if you know what I mean."

"I sure do. Ricky was in the process of painting the house we were sharing. After he was killed, I remember entering the house and the smell of paint and the partially emptied paint cans instantly brought back memories. Even after I had everything removed, I remember one morning making breakfast and felt him there watching me scramble eggs." Jeannie paused and took a sip of wine.

"How long were you married?"

"Six years. The first five were remarkable. While situated in Western Europe, France actually, she insisted on traveling with me to other countries when possible. We toured most of Western Europe. She didn't really like Eastern Europe, so she opted to stay at the home front until my return. All of that changed when she was diagnosed with cancer. She kept putting off seeing a doctor, and I think that allowed the cancer to spread. By the time she saw a physician, it was too late. I put in for a transfer to the states and it was granted. Without a lot of international travel, I could stay close to give her support and care."

Jeannie talked about her first marriage right after college. She felt that the reason for her divorce was because they were both too young. The marriage lasted less than two years, and they handled the divorce through a mediator instead of losing their meager assets to a divorce attorney. She moved in with her parents for a short time, but after the divorce was finalized, she found a new residence.

She promised herself she would never go through a divorce again, and that was her thinking when she married her second husband, Eric, a regional manager for a nationwide sporting goods chain. The money was good and helped them afford Jeannie's continuing graduate education, leading to her doctorate in psychology. They mutually decided to put off starting a family.

She applied for an agent position with the FBI and was accepted. Her basic training lasted twenty weeks, and that put a strain on their marriage. They tried weekend meetings a few times, taking turns visiting each other on opposite coasts, but the arrangement created additional tension since Eric's job demanded that he cover an eight-state area in the west, and Jeannie found she needed weekends to handle her course work and physical training.

She graduated at the top of her class and was initially stationed in the bay area. They told themselves that once together they would have a wonderful marriage and maybe start a family. But, work demands--including Jeannie being sent to the Behavioral Analysis Unit at Quantico for months--further deteriorated their union. Once again, Jeannie found herself a divorced woman.

"I don't know much about the life of an Interpol agent other than what you've told me, but I felt a change in my personality as I became a law enforcement officer. Seeing the worst that humans can do to another made me somewhat cynical and judgmental," Jeannie said.

"Oh, I agree. Maybe not to the extent of an FBI agent, but even in Interpol, we see the worst of humanity," Sean replied.

The conversation turned to their respective childhood and college years. Jeannie loved his accent and loved to kid him about it. He countered by referring to her as "Yank." Dinner was excellent and they decided to split a dessert, followed by Jeannie ordering coffee and Sean opting for tea. Sean used typical English expressions that Jeannie felt would move Ismail to make James Bond related comments were he with them.

Delaney's cell phone rang. He glanced at the number displayed. "This can't be bloody good," he commented to Jeannie before answering, "Delaney." Jeannie sipped more wine, silently warning herself that she still had to drive home across the bay. Hanging up, Delaney looked at Jeannie. "Another kidnapping has just been reported in Munich."

Jeannie called Ismail on her drive home to Newark from the restaurant. Answering the phone, he said, "Hey, where are you? You sound like you're in your car. Are you just now leaving the bureau?"

"Yeah. I'm driving home now." It really wasn't a lie, she told herself. "There was another kidnapping. This one in Munich. Appears to be the same M.O. Victim goes to a club with her girlfriend and then disappears. No witnesses. Delaney is going to get everything he can before tomorrow morning's briefing, but I doubt he'll have anything more."

"Son of a bitch! Either these guys are the luckiest motherfuckers on earth, or they have one hell of an organization. OK, thanks for calling. See you in the morning."

EIGHTEEN

When Jeannie arrived at work the next morning, Delaney had already arrived and was talking with SAC Lomax in the breakroom. "Good morning," she said, feeling her pulse race a little upon seeing Sean.

"Jeannie. Agent Delaney told me they had another one in Germany yesterday, or was it the day before. Can't always calculate the time change. Sounds to me like the same M.O. as the others. I contacted the San Mateo Sheriff, so their abduction is now officially ours. Use as much manpower as you feel necessary. Nice meeting you, Agent Delaney." Lomax topped off his coffee, took a donut and headed back to his desk.

"Did you tell him how great dinner was last night?" Jeannie asked playfully.

"Yes, and I told him you were very professional."

"You didn't talk to him about dinner, did you?" Jeannie asked in panic mode. Sean just winked at her.

Ismail was next to enter the breakroom, followed by Burk. "Late last night we finally finished making copies of all your cases. Sorry Jeannie, but we haven't had the time or energy to review them yet," Burk said, grabbing a Styrofoam cup and filling it with coffee. "Darcy's in her office starting a workup."

"Good," said Jeannie. "But there was another abduction yesterday in Munich." She turned her attention back to Sean. "Were you able to get any more kidnapping information from Europe?"

"Not much, I'm afraid. The victim is in the same age group and her description matches the others. The good news is that we were able to get the security tapes from the club's inside cameras, and we think one of the bartenders put something in her drink since we can see her becoming unsteady on the dance floor a short time later."

"Great!" Jeannie said. "Did the local police pick him up?"

Before Delaney could respond, Ismail jumped into the conversation. "Hey, this might be the missing piece we've needed to solve this case."

"Afraid not, chap. After we reviewed the tapes and began focusing on him, he disappeared. He hasn't shown up for work. They raided his residence, but it had been cleaned out. The rental was paid by several shell corporations and his cell phone was disabled. Like all victims, he's gone. Of course, we're searching bank and cell phone records, and for known associates, but I'm afraid it will lead us down another rabbit hole," Delany said.

"Good morning," Jeannie said, walking to the front of her assembled team carrying a cup of coffee and bagel with cream cheese. "If you're not aware, another kidnapping occurred in Munich yesterday. Before I assign you tasks, Agent Delaney will give you an update about the abduction. Agent Delaney."

Delaney gave the same synopsis he had given in the breakroom. None of the agents asked questions. Jeannie returned to the front and tapped on a computer connected to a screen that had dropped from the ceiling. There, before her team, she shared her thoughts from the night before:

Commonalities	**Dissimilarities**
Age group: 21- 25	
Blonde hair:	Hair length and style
Piercing blue eyes	
5'2 – 5'4"	
Athletic figures	
Abducted	Different locations and times
Most taken from bar--drugged	Few taken from other locations

"Sadly, this is the result of my own brainstorming last night. Please look at my contribution, and as usual, take pot shots at it. Use it to explore other avenues. Bottom line, to date we're no closer to discovering who or what's behind these kidnappings. This has been going on for a long, long time." Silence consumed the room and Jeannie wasn't sure what to say next. Thankfully, Darcy, who was late for the beginning of the briefing, entered.

"Darcy, Agent Delaney gave us an update on the recent Munich kidnapping. I just placed my thoughts on the board. Do you have any questions at this point?" She really didn't expect an answer and was only using the opportunity to delay more fumbling on her part.

"Actually, a light bulb came on in my thoughts while walking here from my office." Darcy looked at Jeannie's list on the screen. "There's actually another commonality." Everyone's attention fell on her and she started to blush.

"Please," Jeannie said.

"It's been facing us all along, but so obvious we probably didn't think to process it. All the females were of German descent. Not a mixture. They're all 100% German." Many in the room turned to the screen and saw that nationality was not indicated on Jeannie's list.

"Huh?" Delaney uttered. "Do you mean to say that the victims here in the U.S. were also of Germanic heritage?"

"Yes. All pure-blooded German," Darcy answered. "That's probably not politically correct, but it's a fact. Every victim you've listed in the Interpol files are of German decent, and I expect last night's kidnapping victim is also German. The same for the Foster City abduction."

Everyone turned their attention from Darcy back to Jeannie. "Thanks Darcy. It was right in front of us!"

Speaking to no one in particular, Ismail interjected, "But I still feel we're missing that one final piece, the one thing needed to start solving this puzzle. Even though the victims share a common nationality, I still can't figure out the motive for the kidnappings. Maybe we should reconsider the cult angle, possibly a cult that only recruits pure blooded Germans."

"Or, as we thought, an international sex-trafficking ring only interested in German women," Delaney added. "I'm afraid Ismail's right. We still need something else."

NINETEEN

Two days later, Jeannie sensed the frustration level rising in her team. Every avenue of approach listed during their brainstorming session had been completely explored, and still they were no closer to breaking the case than they were when the investigation began. To add to her frustration, she had not heard from Sean since the last time he briefed her team about the latest kidnapping. Maybe I read too much into our diner date, she thought. Perhaps it was just two co-workers having a casual meal together.

The Mini Berghain night club is by far the most popular club in Munich, and not just for its gargantuan sound system. Many of the tireless regulars call it a "church." It is extremely popular from Friday midnight until well into Monday morning, especially on Saturday nights. During peak periods, only a third of those waiting in the queue to enter gain entrance. The odds of gaining entrance as a female are only slightly better than for males. Once inside, a zero-tolerance camera ban is enforced, and a patron can expect to be immediately ejected if detected flouting the rules. Other than that, visitors can go wild, safe in the knowledge that nothing they do will ever return to haunt them on social media. That is why Hanna and her girlfriend Lina, liked to party there.

Fortunately for Hanna, Lina knew the gatekeeper this Saturday night and they were allowed easy access to the club, much to the dislike of those who had been standing in line for two hours. As usual, the place was jumping. They went to the bar and ordered a drink before ascending the stairs to the second story dance floor they preferred over the one on the ground floor; the one above played their kind of music. Finding no tables vacant, they began dancing together while holding their drinks. About twenty minutes after finishing her first drink, Hanna knew something was amiss. Confused and not able to find Lina in the crowd, she went downstairs and outside the club, hoping the fresh air would clear her mind.

Suddenly and before she realized what was happening, a black car drove up to the curb and a male jumped out of the front passenger seat and grabbed her right arm. Still in control of her body, she broke free and began to scream. All she could remembered next was the sound of gunshots as she ran toward the crowd waiting to get into the club. This was followed by the sound of others screaming and the sight of the person who tried to grab her lying on the pavement, blood pooling around his body.

Jeannie and Ismail had just returned from lunch and were walking down the hallway toward her office when her cell rang. “Loomis,” she said, having not looked at the caller identification.

“Jeannie, it’s Sean. First, I want to apologize for not calling you sooner. The pressure is mounting around this case and most of our field offices are feeling the heat.”

“Sean. There’s no need to apologize. We’re just as frustrated here over a lack of tangible progress.” Deep inside, however, she was very happy to both hear his voice and the affection it carried. “Nothing new happening?” she asked.

“Actually, yes. There was another attempted kidnapping last night in Munich.”

“You said attempted?”

“What? What happened?” Ismail interrupted.

“It’s Delaney,” Jeannie replied, putting her hand over her cellphone. “There was an attempted kidnapping in Munich.” Removing her hand and speaking directly into the phone, she continued, “Sorry Sean, go ahead.”

“Sean?” Ismail said with a smile on his face. Jeannie hit him on the arm.

“Yeah, a young woman fitting the description of our missing victims was leaving a very popular bar when a black Mercedes approached. We believe she’d been drugged at the bar. Feeling unwell, she went outside to get some fresh air, and that’s when a car approached. A male got out of the front passenger’s seat and grabbed her, but she was able to fight him off and escaped into a crowd of patrons waiting to get into the club. By chance, a constable was nearby and heard her scream as well as the screams of those waiting in line, and when he began to approach the scene, the abductor pulled out a gun and began firing. Fortunately, neither the officer nor any bystander was hit, but the suspect caught two in the chest and was declared dead at the scene.

"His body did not carry any form of identification and we're now awaiting returns on his fingerprints. All we got from the victim was that her attacker only said a few words, and they were spoken in what she perceived as flawless German. Our Munich office is more highly staffed with personnel than we have here in the city, but until we get a return on his identification, I'm afraid we'll just have to hurry up and wait.

"My secretary's in the process of faxing over the reports coming out of Munich to you, and you should receive them shortly." There was a pause, and finally Delaney added that he really wanted to see Jeannie again. Jeannie could not reply with Ismail at her side who was still acting like he had swallowed the canary when she slipped up and said Sean. "Me too," is all she said.

"Sean? Now it's Sean instead of Agent Delaney. Come on boss, spill the beans. Are you interested in 007?"

"Will you behave? We need to let everyone in the team know about this latest attempt."

"This isn't over, boss! Enquiring minds want to know."

TWENTY

"This is number seven, yes?" Dr. Hausser asked the nursing staff assisting him in the latest impregnation.

"Yes, Herr Doctor. "We have two more prepped if you wish to proceed today."

"No. I think I need to rest and finish up with those two tomorrow."

"Very well, Herr Doctor." She looked at another nurse and told her to return the other two subjects to their rooms. She then monitored the stitching of the seventh subject, aware that Hausser was heading to the surgery department's cleanup area. When she was finally able to join him in the post-op room, he had already removed his surgery gown and was only wearing his scrubs.

"Your staff's performance went exceedingly well today, Frau Becker. You and their efforts will go down in history. I was notified late last night that a new subject had to be selected in Berlin and soon we will have the last subject arriving. Tomorrow we will finish with subjects eight and nine, and hopefully by the end of the week number ten will be with us. Soon, very soon after many months of experimenting, we will rejoice with our success." He left the room without waiting for a reply.

Jeannie began the drive home without additional friendly hassling by Ismail. He was still involved with his spider case, at least he had better be, she thought. The final person who was supposed to contact Ismail, Ronald, failed to do so. Ismail was very involved not only with the sex-trafficking case, but was wrapping up two other investigations, so Jeannie gave him some slack regarding the spider investigation.

She was not sure why she was reluctant to tell him about her and Sean's dinner date. Perhaps it was because her dead fiancé, Ricky, was Ismail's cousin. Maybe it was because she didn't know where this possible relationship was going.

Arriving home, she checked her mail and opened her garage door, hoping to avoid Delores. Quickly entering the house, she fed her koi without giving them an update on the case, and then changed clothes. Returning to the garage, she got into her Vette and headed to the local Fish and Chips restaurant. I wonder what a shrink would think about this hidden desire for English food, she thought.

She ordered her favorite: two pieces of cod and a batch of fries plus malt vinegar. That and a diet Dr. Pepper hit the spot. As she was about to take her empty basket to the waste receptable, her cellphone alerted to an incoming call. This time, she checked the caller

ID and saw that it was Sean. Gee, she thought. Here I'm eating a British early dinner and Sean calls. Could this be fate?

"Sean. You'll never guess where I am!"

"Well, I don't hear the sound of traffic, and I learned you'd already left the bureau, but frankly, I don't have any idea. But I think we finally got that missing piece of the puzzle."

The next morning Jeannie arranged for a food preparation company to come to the bureau and make breakfast on demand for her team. Of course, she invited Sean who would discuss the break in the case. At least, she hoped it was a break in the case. It sure sounded positive the night before. After receiving Sean's call at the Fish and Chip restaurant, she immediately called Ismail.

"Hey boss. How's Sean?" he asked, answering the phone.

"Keep it up and you'll never know," she replied. "Listen, Interpol may have gotten a break in the case. The kidnapper fingerprints came back, and get this, he's a modern-day Nazi."

"Nazi? You mean a white supremacy wacko?" Ismail asked.

"Not according to Delaney and Interpol, he's the real thing. He even had what Delaney said was a blood group tattoo on his left armpit. Members of the Waffen-SS were required to have a tattoo on their left arm verifying their blood group," explained Jeannie."

"No shit!" responded Ismail.

"Delaney will be at the bureau the first thing in the morning with more details. I've arranged for Spice Bar to come and prepare breakfast for everyone. I think we'll be busy once we learn what Interpol has found. Can you call half of the team? I'll call the others? Have them in the office by 9:00 a.m. instead of 9:30. This might be that missing piece of the puzzle."

"Not a problem," Ismail said. "I'll have to stop at a grocery store on the way in tomorrow morning if the Spice Bar is going to be there. They never have linguica."

"A true Portugee, aren't you?" Jeannie replied.

A recent report from Hostel World deemed Germany's Hamburg the best place in the world for a night out, ranking it higher than cities like Amsterdam, Berlin and Barcelona. The Ex-Sparr Club was not a high-end nightclub like Berghain in Munich, but for students like Leah and Erika, this place fit the bill. The drinks were cheap, but not watered down. The music was loud enough, but friends could still carry on a conversation; and most importantly, there were lots of men present on weekends.

Max was working the nightshift and at first did not realize his cell was ringing until a co-worker pointed it out. The phone ID showed an unlisted number. He answered, "Max."

"Max," said an familiar voice in German. "The target will be entering the bar in a few minutes. She is wearing a black skirt and blue blouse. She will be with a second female whom we are not interested in. That person is wearing a red pantsuit."

"Understood," Max replied, ending the phone call and focusing his attention on the club entrance. On cue, he saw the target enter, adjusting her eyes to the inside darkness. Although it was 7:00 p.m., daylight savings time provided a sunlit evening.

Max followed their movement while taking care of his bar duties. Neither the target nor her friend approached the bar. There was little he could do but watch and wait. Thirty minutes passed and his cellphone rang again. "Max," he said upon answering.

"Where is the target?" he was asked by the same person who called earlier.

"She is still here, but has not asked for a drink."

"Okay. Call this number once she consumes something."

"Understood."

Finally, after 45 minutes, Max saw the target flirting with a male on the dance floor. The male approached the bar and ordered two drinks. Max placed the GHB in both drinks and stirred them. He gave the drinks to the male and collected the amount due, then watched the male return to the target and offer the drink, which she started to drink. Max pulled out his cell and dialed the number. "She is drinking now."

Everyone seemed to enjoy the breakfast bar in the large briefing room. Even SAC Lomax went back for seconds. Ismail persuaded them to cook his linguica with scrambled eggs and took two pieces of French Toast. Work was not discussed during breakfast. Jeannie sat near Delaney and was aware of Ismail watching. "I remember a professor I had in an undergrad psychology class who said that what we eat affects how we feel. Hopefully this will help fight the frustration we're all feeling," Jeannie said.

"I know I'm feeling better sitting here with you," Sean whispered.

Jeannie felt herself turn several shades of red and knew Ismail noticed. Damn! She thought. "Alright. Did everyone get enough to eat?" she asked, walking to the front of the assembled group.

"Too much!" the SAC replied, causing everyone to laugh.

"As you're aware, Interpol and the German police have been investigating the latest attempted kidnapping. Agent Delaney now has some breaking news regarding their investigation. Agent Delaney."

Jeannie sat next to Ismail who leaned into her and said, "Didn't you mean Sean?"

She poked him in the side.

She overheard two of her newer female agents sitting behind her. "Don't you just love his accent?" one asked.

"Yeah, and he's not bad on the eyes either," came the response.

Jeannie thought to herself, if only you ladies knew.

Delaney tapped his laptop that had been hooked up to a big screen. "Ladies and gentlemen, this was Gunter Muller. I say was, since he is now deceased. He was a 46-years old German national with a long history of criminal activity ranging from robbery to extortion, but that's not the interesting part. The German police have linked him to a group they have never shared with Interpol until now. Muller is believed to belong to a group known simply as The Organization."

Another slide showed a link chart of The Organization with the top person represented by a large question mark. "I'm not sure how much time I have with the team, Agent Loomis, but I do have a lot of information about this group."

"The floor is yours," she said. "Anything you can share might help us aid Interpol in your investigation."

"Yes, thank you. Alright then. How many of you have heard the term Operation Paperclip?"

Only SAC Lomax raised his hand. He looked around, but instead of showing embarrassment, simply said, "Hey, what can I say. I'm old." Laughter filled the room.

"Agent Lomax, can you enlighten the group?" Delaney said, giving him the floor.

"At the end of World War II, orders were given to our top military generals to de-Nazify Germany. It was an Allied initiative to rid German and Austrian society, culture, press, judiciary, and politics of the

Nazi ideology. It was carried out by removing those who had been in the Nazi Party or were SS members from positions of power and influence, and by disbanding organizations associated with Nazism or rendering them impotent.

"Operation Paperclip was a secret program of the United States Joint Intelligence Objectives Agency--now our friends, the CIA--who were largely responsible for more than sixteen-hundred German scientists, engineers, and technicians such as Werner von Braun and his V-2 rocket team. They were brought to the United States for US government employment, primarily between 1945 and 1959. Many were former members of the Nazi Party and some were former leaders.

"Although President Harry Truman officially sanctioned the operation, he forbade the agency from recruiting Nazi members or active Nazi supporters. Nevertheless, officials within the JIOA and Office of Strategic Services known as the OSS, the forerunner to the CIA, bypassed this directive by eliminating or whitewashing incriminating evidence of possible war crimes from the scientists' records, believing their intelligence to be crucial to the country's postwar efforts. Many felt that a war would soon break out between the US and the Soviet Union." Lomax then rose and returned to the buffet table.

"Thank you, Agent Lomax." Delaney said, as he continued. "What many don't know, since the CIA likes to keep a lot of secrets, (laugher filled the room) besides the sixteen-hundred individuals, scientists, engineers and technicians who entered the US, businessmen who ran many of the Nazi programs were also allowed into the country. Some of those Nazis became CEOs of some of our biggest international companies."

"You mean we have Nazis still operating here among us?" asked Darcy.

"Second and third generation, but yes. In fact, about three years ago we investigated a case where the suspect was in his nineties and had been an SS officer assigned to Auschwitz, the death camp." Silence overtook the room.

"Sorry, I've gone off on a tangent, I'm afraid. Under pressure from Interpol, the German authorities reluctantly gave us their information about The Organization. As I stated, it's a large international group of second and third generation Nazis. They're not to be confused with your street-level white supremacy thugs, but actual Nazis, mostly SS. Their hierarchy still follows that used by the SS in World War II. Muller, as you can see on this chart, was not part of the top echelon. He was more of a soldier, certainly not an officer or higher-up in The Organization.

"The Organization controls or is at least a big player in social media, telecom, oil production and distribution, energy, manufacturing, and even farming."

"You mean to tell me that when I'm texting someone, I might be using a company run by a Nazi?" Darcy asked again, still appalled.

"I'm afraid so," came Delaney's reply.

Darcy shook her head and looked at Burk. "This is unbelievable."

Delaney continued, "Sadly, our attempts as well as those of the German police have netted nothing from Muller's home address. His cell phone and records are still being examined. At this stage, we're not even sure Gunter Muller is his real name. The Mercedes was found, but again, it was thoroughly burned. This is what we have so far."

TWENTY-ONE

The seaplane arrived at 3:00 a.m. Leah was still unconscious from several paralytic drug injections administered during her transport from Hamburg. Dr. Hausser did not attend her arrival, leaving it up to the crew that also handled cremations.

Leah was stripped down and given a sponge bath by two nurses assuming responsibility for the great experiment's last needed subject. They drew a sample of her blood as well as swabbed her mouth for a saliva sample, then measured and weighed her as best they could, given she was not yet conscious and unable to support herself. "Herr Doctor will be very happy knowing you are here," a nurse said to the nude female, not expecting a response.

Jeannie was indulging in a hot bubble bath when her cellphone rang. Reaching and retrieving the cell, she saw it was Sean. Thank God this is not a Zoom call, she thought to herself. "Hello, Agent Delaney," she said in a flirtatious manner.

"Hello, Agent Loomis. And how are you this fine evening?"

"Well, your briefing certainly got my team's creative juices flowing again. Darcy and Burk are in overdrive, trying to learn more about The Organization. Darcy's a little pissed and has taken on this case as if it were a crusade. I've heard she's also conducting a private investigation into the ownership of her cell phone carrier and several of the businesses she frequents."

Delaney laughed a little, but then became serious. "Unfortunately, there was another kidnapping. This time in Hamburg."

"Son-of-a-bitch! They're striking quickly. That seems unusual to me," Jeannie said as she slowly got out of the tub, still covered in bubbles.

"Is that water I hear?" Sean asked.

Jeannie blushed, then thought, Oh the hell with it, and said, "Yes, you caught me taking a bubble bath."

"Do you happen to need any help?" he asked.

"Oh, someday that would be nice," she said, smiling to herself. "So, tell me, what happened in Hamburg?"

"Guden morgen, Herr Doctor," the lead surgical nurse said when she saw him enter the hospital. Not bothering to reply, he went directly to his lab coat and put it on.

"The new subject. Is she still sedated?"

"She's in and out of consciousness," the nurse answered. "I believe she received too many injections during transport, but it should wear off within the next few hours."

Dr. Hausser looked at his watch. "We do not have time for indoctrination. When she wakes up, immediately plan on impregnation. We can continue to keep her slightly sedated after the procedure. If she fights us afterward, we will still have nine other suitable candidates."

The next morning, Hausser prepared for the artificial insemination, making an incision into subject number ten. "We are fortunate that our subject here is ovulating, or we could have lost valuable time." He made an incision into her cervix and found her fallopian tubes. The lead surgical nurse began drying his forehead. Hausser looked at a second nurse and nodded. She handed him a syringe containing the donor sperm having the DNA of the Fuhrer. "You, my child, are being blessed with the greatest achievement of thc Fourth Rcich. The resurrection of our great leader, Adolf Hitler."

Having just finished toweling off after her phone call from Sean, her cell went off again. It was Ismail. "Hey, Darcy and Burk have hit a homerun!"

"What? What did they find?" she excitedly asked.

"First, Darcy said to not ask her how she did it, but she was able to access some records held by our nemesis, the CIA."

"Oh God, I hear prison sounds already," Jeannie said.

Ismail continued. "Well, it turns out our buddies over there in Langley know all about The Organization.

Darcy even has the names of major companies set up after World War II and staffed by SS officers who passed the companies off to the next Nazi generation. These latter-day Nazis got into…you name it, manufacturing, education, high-tech, and the list goes on and on. Needless to say, she's really pissed now.

"Now get this! Over the years, these CEOs and their underlings have been trying to re-establish the Third Reich. Actually, they want to create a Fourth Reich. But there's nothing in the files that Darcy accessed that describe how they're attempting to do it."

"Jesus, Mary and Joseph!" Jeannie exclaimed. "What a bunch of sick assholes! Okay. I'll call Delaney and pass on the information. I still don't know what these pricks are up to. Maybe after a good night's sleep it'll come to me. Thanks for the update. See you tomorrow."

She walked into her spare bedroom and looked at the walls. One was dominated by the abducted women's photos, except for the most recent victims. The other wall displayed a copy of the chart Delaney showed of The Organization. "The answer is here. I just can't see it," she said out loud.

She removed The Organization chart and took it downstairs. Spreading it out on the dining room table, she addressed her fish. "Okay guys. Study this chart. After I get myself something to eat, we'll solve this sucker."

Dinner was a frozen Stouffer's Turkey Tetrazzini she tossed into the microwave. While it was heating, she cut a whole wheat roll in two and buttered each half. When the microwave signaled the time was up, she slid the meal onto a dinner plate, placed a fork in the front pocket of her sweatpants and opened the refrigerator. Finding an opened diet Dr. Pepper, she took it out and returned to the table.

"Well. Did you guys solve it?" she asked her koi. She ate some of the TV dinner and glanced from The Organization chart to her koi and back, continuing the exchange until she realized she had finished her meal. Taking her plate to the kitchen still lost in thought, she left it in the sink and returned to the dining room. Maybe I should call Delores, she thought, and immediately broke into a smile.

"Alright. Let's think about this shit," Jeannie said aloud to herself, glancing back and forth from the aquarium to her notes. She began listing what was known to date. "We have a ton of kidnapped women. None have been found alive or dead. Most come from western Europe, with a few coming from the good old U.S.A. We now know that a super-secret group known as The Organization is a bunch of shithead Nazis who our damned government allowed to enter the country after World War II. These bastards now control many of our biggest businesses and are into everything."

Needing a break to clear her thoughts, she began reading a book she bought about koi breeding. She read that in order to breed the best kohaku (red and white koi) with bright red and white markings, one outstanding kohaku female should be placed in a pond or holding facility with three male hohaku displaying the desired characteristics. With this arrangement, the males will compete to distribute their sperm onto the eggs that have been sprayed onto the roots of water hyacinths by the female. Huh! Jeannie thought. Can't call that a three-some. What do you call it? A foursome?"

Looking at her koi, she shook her head and started to think out loud again. "That doesn't get us anywhere, does it? Let's keep going. The Organization wants to re-establish the Third Reich. No, they want to create, what did Ismail say? Oh yeah, the Fourth Reich. Shit! I'm not getting anywhere, and you guys are still no help."

Why the fascination with blonde hair and piercing blue eyes? she thought. Then the proverbial lightbulb went off in her head. "Oh my God!" she burst out loud. She quickly called SAC Lomax.

"Jeannie. Don't tell me they struck again," Lomax immediately said after answering his phone.

"No. You're up to date on the abductions, but I want to pick your brain if you have a few minutes."

"Fire away," he said.

"You seem to know a lot about the Nazis and World War II," she said, hoping to hear an affirmation.

"Just call me a history nut. Plus, as I said at the briefing, I'm old," he replied. "Actually, I learn a lot on the History, Biographies, and National Geographics channels."

"What I recall is that Hitler wanted the Aryan race to dominate the world." Jeannie said. "Last night I saw The Race, the movie about Jesse Owens and the 1936 Olympic games. He single-handedly destroyed Hitler's belief about white supremacy. Am I correct so far?" Jeannie asked.

"It went a lot deeper than that," Lomax answered. "He desired a whole race of blond haired, blue eyed supermen. I also saw that movie. Do you recall the scene where the German track star invites Jesse Owens into his room to have a drink? He told Jesse that a German woman was sent to his room purely to have sex and hopefully become impregnated for the Nazi empire."

"Yes, I remember that scene."

Lomax continued, "They would kidnap children with the desired Aryan look in countries they invaded and give them to SS families to raise. Himmler expanded the program and created Lebensborn, a Nazi breeding program."

"That's it! That's it! Thanks boss. I'll see you in the morning," Jeannie said without letting Lomax know of her sudden breakthrough. She called both Darcy and Burk and gave them an assignment they needed to start working on immediately.

TWENTY-TWO

A restless sleep allowed Jeannie to arrive at the bureau before any of her team. Darcy and Burk were the first team members in. "We think you nailed it Jeannie," said Burk with Darcy nodding yes.

"What did your research reveal?" Jeannie asked.

"The SAC was right. Lebensborn was a massive breeding program established by the SS." Burke said. "It was designed to create racially pure children for the Third Reich. Between 1935 and 1945, the secret program encouraged women whom they thought were racially fit to bear children for the Reich and protected babies they believed to exemplify Nazi Germany's Aryan ideology. Translated as fountain of life, the Lebensborn program involved secret birthing facilities, hidden identities, and the kidnaping of hundreds of thousands of children throughout Europe, especially in occupied territories where the Nazis thought the populous had an Aryan look."

"Jesus!" Jeannie exclaimed.

"It gets worse," Darcy said, before continuing. "Because the population birth rate declined in western

Europe just before and after World War I, especially in Nazi Germany, Hitler had a problem. His plans to usher in a new world order in which Nordic and Germanic Aryans, whom they considered the most superior of the races, would rightfully reign supreme, but he was coming up short number-wise. To carry out his vision of a completely Aryan Europe, the Nazis had to address the need of the country's genetic shortage.

"The head of the SS, Heinrich Himmler, put the blame for the birth rate decline on abortionists. So, he made abortions of racially pure children less appealing by offering an alternative to their mothers. Women who could prove that their unborn child would fit Nazi racial purity standards could give birth in a secret and comfortable facility."

"Why did Hitler put Himmler in charge of the program?" Jeannie asked.

"Various opinions are out there," Darcy answered. "Whether any of them are correct, who knows. Most historian believe that Himmler's experience raising excellent chickens on his farm led Hitler to believe he was qualified to oversee the breeding program."

"But now get this," Burk added. "There was a catch. Once the babies were born, they had to be relinquished to the SS. The SS would then educate them, indoctrinate them in Nazi ideology, and give them to elite families to raise."

"At first, Himmler urged the SS and German military to have children with Aryan women both in and out of wedlock, but as the war progressed, that became a mandate. When casualties further decimated the German male population, Himmler ordered his officers to marry and reproduce. Women in occupied countries were also encouraged to have children with German soldiers.

"As invasions moved eastward, the Third Reich expanded the Lebensborn program to include wholesale kidnapping. Children thought to be racially pure were taken from their parents and temporarily placed in Lebensborn homes before being adopted by German families. In Poland alone, between one-hundred and two-hundred thousand children were kidnapped; those who failed racial purity tests in Germany were sent to orphanages or summarily executed."

"That is what Lomax told me last night. My God! How many children did they breed?" Jeannie asked.

"No one really knows," replied Darcy. "Current estimates range up to sixty-thousand. However, that number may never be fully known due to secrecy on the part of mothers, incomplete or destroyed records, and new names given to children who were placed in Nazi families."

"That's it! This is not a sophisticated sex-trafficking ring, serial killers or even a cult. The Nazis are starting Lebensborn all over again." Jeannie said. "Let's brief the rest of the team."

Delaney and Ismail were the next to arrive and entered the office together. Delaney, carrying several boxes of donuts said, “I believe this is the required breakfast for American law enforcement,” as he laid them on Jeannie’s desk.

“Jolly good,” Burk said in a fake British accent as he began reaching for one of the boxes.

“Bloody hell!” Delaney exclaimed. “I believe that’s the worst British accent I’ve ever heard.”

Burk blushed while carrying the boxes from Jeannie’s office to the breakroom. Everyone else laughed. While everyone was getting seated, Darcy’s phone went off. She excused herself, telling Jeannie she was expecting an important phone call. Jeannie didn’t ask who from.

Jeannie, Burk, and Delaney filled everyone in on the latest findings. Burk left out how Darcy had gotten the information. Darcy excitedly ran back into the room with a flash drive in her hand. “Must be good,” Jeannie said. Darcy took over the floor without asking for permission. Jeannie loved it when one of her team members was on a roll.

“I just received some information from a reliable source,” she said, avoiding Jeannie or SAC Lomax.

Jeannie whispered to Lomax, “Don’t ask.”

Darcy placed the drive into the computer’s USB port and the image of an elderly, but in good shape, white male with dark hair appeared. “This is Dr. Wolfgang Hausser,” she said. My source said he’s not the head of The Organization, but near the top. He’s a geneticist and originally from Germany. He disappeared many years ago while being investigated for the illegal cloning of animals. Get this, his father worked with the Angel of Death, Joseph Mengele at Auschwitz."

"That's it! Jeannie yelled," rising from her seat. She looked at Delaney who also stood and began reaching for his phone. "They're using the victims for cloning," she said.

"Cloning what? New little Nazis?" Darcy asked.

Jeannie could not hear what Delaney was saying into his phone, but when he got off, he raised his hand, requesting quiet in the room. "I think Doctor Hausser and The Organization has something far more sinister planned. Interpol just received information that the remains of Adolf Hitler were stolen from a safe in Moscow. They're planning on cloning and bringing back their Fuhrer."

"Is that even possible?" Darcy asked. "I mean, I know about Dolly and the cloning of some animals, but cloning a human, and using Hitler's DNA?" No one offered an opinion. Instead, they just stared at each other.

Delaney gave a full account of what his agency had learned about the theft. The Russians, of course, denied any theft and stated they were still in possession of the items. "To say they were uncooperative would be an understatement," he said.

"So, where do we go from here?" Ismail asked to no one in particular. Jeannie looked at Delaney who looked back at her, and then to Ismail, Burk and Darcy.

"Does Interpol have any information as to where Hausser might be?" Jeannie asked.

"We're now turning all of our attention to him. Hopefully, something will come of it," Delaney replied.

"It's an awfully big world out there, and with The Organization's financial support at his beckoning call, he could be anywhere," Ismail said, finishing off his cup of coffee and donut.

TWENTY-THREE

Calls to the Berlin police department came from multiple sources. Gun shots had been heard in the eastern section of the city with one person reported dead and another wounded and being treated by witnesses. A police officer, who by chance was in the immediate vicinity, shot the shooter. A second unit arrived and found a male in his mid-forties dead from two gunshot wounds, one in the head and one in the chest. A younger male was sitting and holding his shoulder while a female was applying some sort of bandage with the assistance of the first officer at the scene.

Witnesses told the police that a car drove past the younger male and suddenly stopped. The now deceased got out of the car and approaching him, pulled out a handgun and began firing. The younger male was wounded, but before the assassin could finish the job, a police officer shot and killed him on the spot.

Further investigation found that the younger male was named Max Luther. Running his name through the computer system resulted in a hold placed by both the Berlin police and Interpol.

The next morning Jeannie and Ismail arrived in the bureau's parking garage simultaneously. "Hey boss. How's double-o-seven?" Ismail teased.

"OK. Let's get this over with. It's Delaney, not Sean, and I did have dinner with him one time several weeks ago. There you go. There's nothing more to say."

"So, you say! We shall see. Remember, I'm a highly trained FBI agent."

As soon as they arrived on their floor, Jeannie's secretary said that the SAC wanted to see them both ASAP. "I sure hope there wasn't another kidnapping," Ismail said.

They found Lomax on his phone when they arrived at his office door. He waved them in, pointing to two chairs across from his desk. "Thank you. Yes, we can take it from here." Ending his call, he turned to the two of them, focusing on Jeannie. "Jeannie, get your passport and suitcase. Washington has given approval for you to fly to Germany and assist Delaney and Interpol."

"Does Delaney know?" Jeannie asked.

"He's the one who put in the request after running it through me. Your flight leaves in less than five hours. Make me proud but be careful. Ismail, once again you'll take over Jeannie's position. You're still investigating that spider case, correct?"

"Oh yeah, I'm all over it," Ismail responded. Jeannie had a smile that only Ismail could see.

Jeannie called Delaney and they agreed to meet at the SFO food court since she had not had a chance to eat and was famished. He did not go into much detail on the phone other than to say that Max was being held for them to interview.

Jeannie contacted the legal department and requested that they take care of the documents she would need to fly with her weapon internationally. She arrived home in record time and began packing her suitcase. She found her passport and realized she did not know when she would be returning. For once, she hoped Delores would be home. Busybody or not, she and her husband were always dependable.

Delores answered her door on the second knock. "Jeannie, is everything alright?"

"Yes, but I need to fly to Germany in a few hours and I'm wondering if you could take care of my fish and garbage can while I'm gone?"

"Germany. Wow! What type of case are you working on that requires you to fly to Germany?"

Jeannie smiled and decided to have a little fun. "Actually, we're chasing real-life Nazis."

"Nazis! My word. I thought we got rid of those bastards during the war. Sorry for my language. Well look, never mind about your fish or the garbage being taken out on time. Walter and I would love to take care of it. Just promise me you'll be safe."

Jeannie parked in a slot designated for law enforcement at the airport and left a business card saying her return may be extended, and if there were a problem to call SAC Lomax at the same number.

Delaney was waiting for her outside the food court. Before ordering they checked in at the TSA station, presenting their service weapons related documents and placed them in a secured box which would travel with them to and from Hamburg.

The eighteen and half-hour flight for Jeannie was nearly unbearable. There was a crying baby in the row directly behind her and a snoring gentleman in the adjacent seat. Scheduling a direct flight with such short notice prevented them from sitting next to each other. Delaney ended up about thirteen rows behind Jeannie.

Upon arrival, the two opted to get their weapons from the TSA first, and then proceed to the luggage carousel since they still had a fifteen-minute wait before their suitcases would come down the shoot. With a restroom stop taken care of, they exited the airport in search of their Interpol driver. Outside, they found a drizzly foggy day in Germany.

Delaney's cell rang. He took it while looking for their driver. A few moments later, a BMW approached and hit them with high and then low headlight beams. Jeannie looked at Delaney who pointed to the BMW while finishing his call. Jeannie got into the back seat and Delaney rode next to the driver, telling him their destination as they pulled away from the curb. Delaney turned around to Jennie, "I'm afraid we'll have to go directly to the Hamburg police station and interview the suspect. They have some rule that a suspect can only stay in their housing facility a few days, at which point a suspect must be transferred to a detention center."

TWENTY-FOUR

The Hamburg Police Department consisted of twenty-four boroughs, plus one at the airport and another at the train station. Max was being held at the borough nearest downtown Hamburg, close to where the shooting took place. Although the police department's ranking structure was similar to that in the US, the prosecutor's office actually ran the department. "I'm sure he'll be there when we arrive," Delaney said. "I must warn you that even after all these post World War II years, the Germans are very sensitive about investigations that involve Nazis. To be honest, I wouldn't be surprised if some of them are on the force, or in the prosecutor's office."

"Gee. Nothing like going in a little blind," Jeannie said from the backseat.

"Quite right, I'm afraid. We'll have to 'play the game' as they say. Here we are." Delaney told the driver to wait, having no idea how long it would be before they returned. They entered the building and identified themselves to the woman officer at the desk. She welcomed them and said the prosecutor would be with them shortly. A few minutes later a stout, aggressive looking middle-aged male wearing wire rim glasses approached with outstretched hand.

"Hello, I am Wilhelm Schmidt. I am the prosecutor assigned to this borough." Following handshakes, he added, "Please follow me." They entered a mid-sized office obviously set up for three people. Various law books decorated one wall, and a presumed map of the local borough hung on another. The prosecutor took his seat and motioned for Jeannie and Delaney to take the two chairs opposite him. A German flag in its stand dominated one corner of the room.

"I have only a limited amount of information regarding your investigation, Agent Delaney," he said. Schmidt did not seem overly friendly, and only briefly acknowledged Jeannie's presence. "So, perhaps you can shed a little light on what type of investigation you are involved in, and also explain why an FBI agent is here with you here in Hamburg?"

"We're investigating a large number of women who have been kidnapped, primarily here in Western Europe, but in the United States as well." Avoiding the mentioning of anything Nazis or The Organization related, Delaney hinted they were investigating the possibility of a sophisticated sex-trafficking ring."

"And why do you suspect the subject we have in custody is part of that ring?" he asked.

"Most of the female abductions have occurred in nightclubs where victims have been given a date-rape drug. When the women wander outside for fresh air, a waiting team of suspects kidnaps them. To date we have over thirty missing women," Delaney replied.

"Well, yes, our suspect is employed as a bartender. Whether he gave the victim any illegal drug has not been confirmed." Schmidt stared at Delaney who wasn't sure if Schmidt believed his outline of their investigation. He then turned his attention to Jeannie. "And how does this involve the FBI?" Jeannie stated that as indicated by Agent Delaney, since several of the women came from the US, it fell under FBI jurisdiction.

"I see," Schmidt said. "Very well, you may interview the suspect. I think you will find him very uncooperative. He will be handcuffed to a desk when you enter. I assume you are both armed, so you must leave your service weapons with the officer outside my office." He stood and escorted them outside, pointing to the officer at the desk. Stating something in German, the officer took out two metal boxes and waited for the two to hand him their weapons. Each were given a key with a number corresponding to each box.

After securing the boxes in a larger safe, the officer rose and walked the two to an interview room where they saw Max sitting handcuffed to a desk. The room was approximately 10' by 10' and only had two additional chairs for Delaney and Jeannie. Max gave Delaney a glance but concentrated on Jeannie.

Speaking in German, Delaney, asked Max if he spoke English. Max did not respond, so Delaney continued addressing him in German. Jeannie could decipher that

Sean was identifying her. Max continued to stare only at Jeannie until Delaney mentioned the FBI.

"FBI. From the United States?" Max asked in English. Obviously, he knows English, Jeannie thought to herself.

"Yes, the Federal Bureau of Investigation from the United States," answered Delaney. Looking at Jeannie and speaking in English, Max asked if any of them were Jewish swine? Jeannie felt that this was Max's attempt to get a reaction from them. Neither Jeannie nor Delaney answered.

Delaney asked Max if he was a Nazi? Max transferred his focus from Jeannie to Delaney and proudly said that he was. He then turned back to Jeannie.

"And you. Miss FBI. How could your citizens ever elect a nigger for your President?" he said before laughing out loud. "You could not elect an Aryan to lead your nation? Even your President Clinton who chased pussy even in the White House, had more class than your Obama. Now, your new President, President Trump, this man is not afraid to say what is on his mind. He takes everyone on and never backs down. He is like Putin. Why are there some in your country that get upset when your president wants your country to be great again? That is what a great leader wants for his people."

Not wanting their interview to trail off into a political debate, Delaney asked Max to tell them about what happened the other night when he got shot.

"What? It is nothing but a scratch."

"The doctors said a few inches either way, and you could have been killed," Delaney responded. Max shook his head from side-to-side and continued to look at Jeannie.

Jeannie decided it was her turn to match wits with this Nazi. "Max, we came a long way to meet with you and we don't want to waste your time or ours. So instead of asking you questions which you will avoid answering, let me tell you a story." Max leaned back in his chair and grinned.

"I will not answer any questions until you tell me if either of you are Jews."

Jeannie started again. "First Max, since that's so important to you, the answer is no, neither I nor Agent Delaney are Jewish. We are investigating a large number of women who've been kidnapped both here in Europe and in the United States. What's remarkable, is that each woman looks almost identical to the others who are missing--like me, with blonde hair and blue eyes." Max smiled, but did not respond.

"This is what we believe," continued Jeannie. "These young ladies liked to party, so they went to their local nightclubs hoping to have a good time. There, a bartender placed a drug in their drink, making them drowsy. They wandered outside for fresh air where kidnappers took them away." Jeannie noticed Max's eyes dart back and forth when she mentioned bartender.

"So, what has that to do with me?" he asked smugly.

"I'm not through with my story Max, and as I promised you, I'm not asking questions, am I? You see Max, we initially thought this was all about an international sex trafficking ring. Boy were we off base!" she said, looking at Delaney. "This is something much bigger, much more elaborate, with far reaching consequences for the world. Agent Delaney, my voice is kind of raspy. You know, our long flight, the lousy plane food. Perhaps we can take a break so I can get something to drink. Would you like something Max?"

At first, Max did not respond, and Jeannie knew he was processing the information she had presented, wondering how much Jeannie knew. Finally, Max requested a soda--either a Coke or Pepsi.

"So, what do you think?" Delaney asked Jeannie after exiting the room and walking toward a vending machine.

"I think that if we proceed like we're doing, Max will rollover and give up some valuable information. Remember, in The Organization, he is only a low hanging fruit. I think we can use his attempted assassination as a means of opening him up. As he was talking, I realized he's our only possible chance of getting inside The Organization. If he shuts down, our case once again comes to a shrieking halt. Let's get him a soda and maybe even a candy bar. I could go for one myself," Jeannie said. After making their purchases, they returned to the interview room.

"Max, I'm almost finished with my story. I hope I'm not boring you."

"Hey, you flew all the way here to Hamburg. Use all the time you want, FBI," he said, smiling and sipping his Pepsi.

"Oh, I forgot. I got you a candy bar." She pulled the bar from her pocket and placed in front of Max. "I don't know when you may ever get another one," Jeannie said while continuing to slide the Hershey bar across the table to Max, who stopped it and began to remove its wrapper. No thank you was given.

"Now, where was I? Oh, yes. Back to you. What the German police told us is that witnesses saw you come out of the bar. Records show you just got off work. You walked to a corner and stopped to light a cigarette and took a few drags. A black car slowed down, and a man got out of the passenger side of the car. You recognized him and started walking toward him until you saw him pull out a gun and began shooting at you. You got hit. Fortunately, the gunman wasn't able to run up and finish you off because there was a police officer already in the area who saw the shooting go down. That police officer saved your life by shooting and killing your assailant. The car, with at least one other person inside, drove off." Jeannie stopped and allowed Max to think about what was said.

"Again, as promised, I still don't have any questions for you, but I do want to be honest. We know a lot about you and The Organization." Jeannie allowed the mentioning of The Organization to hang in the air. For the first time, both she and Delaney noticed sweat on Max's upper lip. He tried to drink more soda but had already finished the can. He tried to bring saliva to his mouth but could not produce any--all classic signs a trained forensic psychologist such as Jeannie or a polygraph examiner would notice as deception.

TWENTY-FIVE

Entering hour two with Max, Jeannie began feeling the effects of jet lag. She found her thoughts ranging from wanting to sleep to being caressed by Sean. After a second break, Jeannie started the interrogation. "Max. There's a final story I want to share with you. Years ago, my team was investigating a secretive urban terrorist group that called themselves the Sons and Daughters of Liberty. This was a reference to those individuals who helped form the United States during our American Revolution. They were a group of assassins who carried out the sentences of a clandestine court known as the Star Chamber. They also conducted a high-profile child kidnapping as well as killing members of the Star Chamber with a bomb. My purpose for telling you this story is that we finally caught the leader of this group. He was tried and convicted in our courts and given a life sentence. He thought that in prison, he would be acknowledged for his deeds, but instead, a gang brutally killed him." Jeannie omitted saying that this same group was responsible for the death of her fiancé.

It was Delaney's turn. "Max, we know that the people who tried to kill you were members of The Organization. Anyone they feel are expendable, or as we call them, 'loose ends,' are eliminated. If you don't cooperate with us, you'll undoubtedly be placed in a German prison. Even if a Nazi gang exists inside whom you think will protect you, you will not be safe. As Agent Loomis just told you, one way or the other, they will get you. You will be killed."

Max fidgeted in his chair, shifting his gaze back and forth between Delaney and Jeannie. "And what can you do for me? You are not German." We got him, Jeannie thought. Immediately pouncing on this opening, Delaney told him that Interpol was a global law enforcement agency. Both his agency and the FBI would inform the German authorities of his cooperation in helping them locate the missing women. They would recommend a light sentence in a detention facility that could insure his life.

Max did not respond. He looked at both agents and then his hands. "I need to see what you are offering in writing. If you put down what you just promised, I will cooperate. I will tell you everything that I know, but first I need something the eat."

Jeannie and Delaney should have been exhausted, but they got a second wind from what Max had just revealed. Jeannie phoned Darcy and gave her the names Max gave up during interrogation. Delaney called the main branch of Interpol, requesting all the information they had on a Dr. Wolfgang Hausser and the names that Jeannie had given to Darcy. A kindly Hamburg police officer gave Jeannie and Delany the name of a restaurant he thought they might enjoy, and they had their driver drop them off. Delaney told the driver to go home and that he would arrange for another driver to pick them up after they finished dinner.

The restaurant was more of a hof brau, offering sandwiches with a choice of pastrami, turkey, roast beef, tri-tip, baked ham and corned beef. Naturally, sauerkraut was offered as an add on. "I can't believe that in the twenty-first century, the ideas of Nazism are still alive and well," Delaney said before taking a drink from the largest mug of beer he had ever seen. "I'm concerned about the fate of all of those missing women. If The Organization eliminates any person they feel expendable, I shudder to think what happened to those who have been part of their experiment."

"With the exception of those still being held, I believe we'll find they've all been killed. As I see it, the question now, it's his location," Jeannie responded. After living on candy bars and sodas for the better part of the day, dinner fit the bill. They skipped coffee but did share a toast over a glass of schnapps which only Delaney seemed to enjoy.

Jeannie's cell rang. It was Darcy. "Jeannie, I think we have the possible whereabout of Hausser. I got into another classified document and found that during their last investigation into The Organization, Hausser was living on an unnamed island off the coast of Argentina. The NSA is working on the exact location from the directions given in the document. Don't worry. I was very discrete about whom I'm working with, since through my investigation I've learned that The Organization has it tenacles into nearly all major businesses. Also, Dr. Hausser's great-grandfather was Joseph Mengele, the 'Angel of Death' as he was known in Auschwitz. Looks like Hausser continued with his great-grandfather's experiments, trying to create a master Aryan race."

"More than that Darcy," said Jeannie, "He's trying to bring back the number one Nazi of them all."

"Oh my God! You mean Hitler? I was able to get photos of the doctor from a file. I'll send them to you right now."

Following Darcy's call, Jeannie and Delaney went to their respective rooms to get some sleep. Jeannie had visions of being in Delaney's room, in his arms and in his bed, but the two were exhausted.

At 4:10 a.m., Jeannie found herself wide awake for no apparent reason. She tossed and turned, trying to go back to sleep, but could not. Finally, she got up and headed toward the shower; she was too tired to do so before going to bed. Glancing at the nightstand clock she saw that it was only 4:40. She had planned to meet Delaney in the hotel breakfast area at 7:00, so she pondered how to pass the next several hours.

What the hell. Why not explore downtown Hamburg and do some window shopping, she thought.

Dressed as warmly as she could with what she brought with her and hoping she would not need an umbrella, she grabbed her purse and started toward the door; but then realized she had almost forgotten her phone. Quickly picking it up, she slid it into her rear pants pocket instead of her purse. On her way out, she politely nodded at the hotel lobby attendant and left. It was chilly out with a slight mist in the air, reminiscent of the climate in San Francisco she thought. The area leading west from the hotel looked the most promising, so she set off in that direction. Many of the stores had been long closed for the night, but their overnight window display lights provided enough illumination for her to look at the merchandise on display.

Crossing the street, she set out for the next block of stores. The first one displayed mostly tourist items sporting Hamburg landmarks. Jeannie thought that if she had time, she would pick up a few items for Ismail, Lomax, Burk, Darcy and her secretary. Lost in thought about what would be appropriate for each of them and trying to decide how she and Delaney should proceed with the case, she did not notice that a male dressed in black was concealed in an alley way until it was too late. The last thing she remembered was the sound of electricity and someone lowering her to the ground.

TWENTY-SIX

Still groggy, the first thing Jeannie could comprehend was that the seat she was strapped into was vibrating and the sound of airplane engines. Becoming more alert, she realized her hands had been cuffed behind her back and the plastic cuff was irritating her wrists. She tried to move them back and forth, hoping there might be some forgiveness in their hold, but there was none.

At least two people were communicating in German in the cockpit She was the only person in the second row of seats. She must have made enough movement to attract her kidnappers attention, because the front passenger turned around, smiled at her and said, "Hello, Ms. FBI agent. And how do you like your flight so far?"

"Why don't you come back here and take my cuffs off, Asshole, and I'll show you how much I love your accommodations."

"Now, now. We have a long trip ahead of us, so don't let your temper do something you will regret."

"Fuck you and your Nazi buddy flying this plane."

"Very well. Have it your way," he replied as he quickly gave Jeannie another electric shock from his Taser. "Sleep tight, Ms. FBI."

Jeannie did not answer her hotel room's phone when Delaney called from the dining area after she failed to show up for breakfast. He went to her room and knocked on the door, thinking she might have overslept. Getting no response, he headed downstairs, hoping that somehow he missed her. Not finding her there either, he checked with the front desk.

"No sir. I have not seen a lady matching your description. I just came on duty at six this morning."

"Can you get me the manager?" Delaney asked.

"He will not be in until eight o'clock," the receptionist replied.

Delaney pulled out his credentials and told her this was a possible emergency, and for her to get the manager on the phone. After explaining the situation to the manager, he was granted access to Jeannie's room as well as having the receptionist call the off-duty person whom she relieved.

It appeared that most of Jeannie's clothes were in her room, or at least there were clothes left behind and her laptop was still there. Wet towels in the bathroom suggested she had been there a short time before, and it looked as though she had used her makeup. There were no signs of a struggle.

The phone in her room rang and Delaney answered, hoping it was Jeannie. "Jeannie? Where are you?" he said.

"Sorry sir, this is Helmut. I was the front desk person last night. I did see your female friend leave the hotel around 4:40 or so. I did not notice what direction she went after she left, and I did not see anyone with her."

Panic now set in. Delaney could not calculate the current time in San Francisco and he did not care. Lomax answered after several rings. "Sir, we have a problem. Jeannie's missing from the hotel and I fear she's been abducted."

Ismail activated his car's red lights and siren to expedite his travel to the bureau. All he could think of was Lomax's words on the phone that Jennie might have been kidnapped. Blond hair, blue eyes. Over and over, the same questions ran through his mind. No, she doesn't fit the age profile. If these are the suspects we're looking for, they took her for some other reason.

Burk and Darcy beat Ismail to the office. "We know where she is," Burk said as soon as he saw Ismail.

"Great. How? Where was she?"

"No, sorry. I meant that Darcy has been able to track her cellphone."

Darcy looked up from her computer screen with Lomax looking over her shoulder. "Looks like they're leaving Frankfort and flying toward Italy," she said.

Lomax pressed a button on his cellphone and connected with Delaney. "Sean, we have her signal. They're traveling from Frankfort heading toward Italy. These assholes didn't file a flight plan, so God knows where they're taking her," and after a pause, he continued. "Yes, she's here. Let me give her my phone." He handing the phone to Darcy while Burk, Ismail, and now Lomax speculated about what Darcy and Delaney were discussing.

Finishing her conversation, Darcy handed the phone back to Lomax and filled them in. "Okay, Delaney's now using Interpol resources to track the plane. I also gave him the name of my CIA contact and hopefully they can assist--off the books of course. The plane will have to land somewhere in Italy for refueling, but like Delaney said, God knows where. His gut and mine tell us they're heading to South America."

Turning to Lomax, Darcy said, "Sir, he said to expect an urgent phone call from him in about thirty minutes." Lomax nodded and left the three alone as he returning to his office. Ismail, Burke, and Darcy stared at each other.

"Shit! What can we do?" Ismail asked. The two walked around behind Darcy and saw the beep coming from the aircraft on her computer screen.

Lomax's answered his phone on its first ring. "Lomax."

"Delaney here, sir. I need to provide you with some delicate and confidential information, information we hope does not go public. Interpol has a secret branch, our S-Branch if you will. This top-secret division is rarely used in hopes of keeping it secret from enemies both foreign and domestic. We feel it rivals your US Navy Seals, but who is to say. The reason I'm bringing this matter up with you sir, is to let you know what's going on behind the scenes. With the information Darcy and her contact inside the CIA provided, the S-Branch has now been able to track the plane by satellite. Our field offices have been alerted to monitor all airports and refueling stops the suspects may use. Assuming we're correct in suspecting their final destination is somewhere in South America, I believe they're taking her to the island we're been searching for. I've been authorized to mobilize the S-Branch, and we're heading to the Buenos Aires Airport as I speak. Should their plane land somewhere else in Argentina, we'll be prepared to launch from there."

"Okay." Lomax said. "If you need anything from our agency, just ask. Keep me in the loop."

TWENTY-SEVEN

The plane shook upon landing, awaking Jeannie. She had a splitting headache and surmised it was from the electric Taser jolts she received. "Ms. FBI agent. We have arrived. How is your head? I decide to not continue shocking you. If you feel pain in your neck, it is from a hypodermic injection to keep you sedated. You really need to do something about your temper."

Jeannie could see through the window that their landing strip was nothing more than a dirt road surrounded by rows and rows of sunflowers. "Now, Ms. FBI, I can give you another shot of electricity and then another shot of the good stuff, or you can be still for the remainder of the flight. We have almost reached our destination." Jeannie did not like either of his offerings and said she would comply with his demand.

After refueling, they were back in the air. Jeannie hoped the earlier vibration from her cell phone was not heard over the plane's prop noise. She had been in panic mode while the plane was on the ground for fear it would ring. Although she was sitting on it and the vibration sound emanating from an incoming call would have been muted, it could have been heard by both the pilot and the man with the Taser.

A several hours later, Jeannie could see that the plane was flying over a large body of water. The plane began to lower its altitude. "We are finally here," the pilot said to his two passengers. He banked the plane and it continue to circle over what appeared to be an inlet. Jeannie thought it would have been considered beautiful by someone who had not been kidnapped.

A few bounces on the water and the plane landed and began its approach to the dock where a small native boy was waiting with mooring ropes. Once the plane had been secured, the passenger in the front pointed the Taser at Jeannie, and with a knife in his other hand cut the cuffs on her feet and wrists. "Okay, Ms. FBI, lets meet someone who is very interested in you."

It took several minutes for Jeannie to regain feeling in her arms and legs. Once she regained her balance, the man who had previously held the Taser helped her out of the plane. The pilot was now holding an automatic that Jeannie thought was a Glock. Next to the dock awaited a red Jeep truck and driver. The pilot climbed into the front passenger seat and the other sat in the back with Jeannie.

The heat was so unbearable that Jeannie felt she might faint. She could feel her blouse clinging to her back as sweat began to form on her forehead and in her cleavage. The wind coming through the Jeep's openings during the drive up a small hill only brought a small amount of relief. Jeannie could see during the drive that the final destination appeared to be a huge villa atop a hill. She heard the calls of Macaws in the background and could finally see them in the trees as the Jeep approached the house.

The gun toting passenger escorted Jeannie out of the Jeep. Using the weapon, he pointed to the front door which was already open. Several large fans operating on high speed provided welcomed relief from the outdoor heat. A servant girl came with a silver plate containing numerous glasses of what appeared to be juice. Jeannie took one and thanked her.

"Sit, and be still," one of the kidnappers said to Jeannie, pointing to one of three couches arranged in a U-shape. A few minutes later, Jeannie heard a door close and saw an elderly male wearing white pants, white loafers, and a white button-down shirt and in good shape staring at her as he made his way down the stairs. He never took his eyes off Jeannie until he reached the bottom. He waved at the person with the gun to put it away. "Special Agent Jeannie Loomis of the San Francisco, FBI," he said, looking at her.

"And you must be Wolfgang Hausser, the sick doctor who's trying to clone another sick bastard, Adolf Hitler," she replied.

"I see the FBI has done its homework," he said. Hausser had a smile on his face as he walked closer to Jeannie. She did not expect the slap across her face and the speed of delivery. Her eyes began to water, but she immediately returned her stare at Hausser.

"Is that how you get your rocks off? Slapping ladies?"

"Too bad Special Agent Loomis. If you were what, fifteen to twenty years younger, your body could have been used to create the greatest leader of the twenty-first century. You have all the characteristics I desire. Blond hair, blue eyes, athletic body. It is a shame. Unlike other females that my colleagues procured for my studies, you are too old."

The sting of the slap started to subside. "You want to bring back a monster who killed millions of men, women, and children?"

"Yes, millions were exterminated, but they were inferior human beings. They were not Aryan. They used up the planet's valuable resources. Look at your own nation. You have allowed inferior humans to occupy seats of power, and what has it given you. Faggots, transvestites, drug addicts, and I could go on."

"So, what's the plan, Hausser?" Jeannie asked, deliberately not giving him the title of doctor. "You will create a clone of Hitler and wait thirty to forty years for him to recreate his Third Reich? A lot can happen in thirty years. Some of our radical politicians believe the world will come to an end by then due to global warming, or whatever narrative they are currently using."

"Not the Third Reich, but a new and glorious Fourth Reich," Hausser exclaimed. "True, I will not be around to see the culmination of my experiment, but members of The Organization will pave the way for his entrance into the world of leadership. Sadly, you will not be here to witness it either I am afraid."

A male hurriedly entered the room from what appeared to be a patio area. He walked up to Hausser and whispered something into his ear. "I'm afraid we will have to continue our little talk later. I have things I must attend to before my guests arrive. Put her upstairs in the holding room in the hospital. You will excuse me," he said, walking to the patio. "Once I have time, we will talk again, about how your agency was able to find me."

"Drop dead fascist. I won't tell you shit."

"Oh, yes you will, Agent Loomis. We have even better ways of extracting information than the SS of old. But I think I will personally use the older methods on you. It will be more enjoyable."

TWENTY-EIGHT

The two men from the plane escorted Jeannie from the villa to the hospital. She noticed the huge SS flag flying over the entrance. They took an elevator to a room with barred windows and left, locking the door behind them. Jeannie went to the only window and looked down on what appeared to be an outdoor patio area. She heard the sound of planes overhead. Maybe her rescue. She could only hope.

She took her cell from the rear pocket of her pants, knowing there would be no reception. She just hoped that someone had tracked her at least to the general area of the island. Not wanting the phone discovered, she placed it in the middle of the bed's top mattress and box springs. Come on Burk and Darcy. Do your magic and let everyone know where the hell I am, she thought to herself.

The first of many seaplanes began arriving at noon. Several vehicles shuttled arriving guests up from the docking area to the hospital where they were greeted by high-ranking SS personnel who directed them to the patio area. The weather was very warm, but not extremely humid. Many guests stopped and admired the flora that surrounded the path up to the hospital as well as the numerous Macaws "talking" to them as they passed.

Although Jeannie was only able to open the window about two inches, she could hear laugher and classical music. She saw numerous individuals arrive at the patio and could see several tables upfront with chunks of lobster, skews of BBQ shrimp, balls of brown meat, salads, fruit, and glasses of champagne. On a smaller table were numerous Cuban cigars still in their little glass containers.

The walls were decorated with large red Nazi flags as well as flags displaying the SS emblem. An immense photo of Adolf Hitler in a brown military uniform hung in the center of the largest wall. Women were dressed in clothing suitable for a ballroom extravagant, while most men wore loose fitting slacks and button-down shirts. Other males at the perimeter wore black SS uniforms with traditional highly polished boots. Dr. Hausser was not among them.

Back at his main residence, Hausser was climaxing inside a young white Aryan semi- conscious female whom he had referred to for several months as subject number four. "You know my dear, it is said that before you give a presentation, it is best to become completely relaxed. Bull fighters I am told have sex before battling their bulls." Finished, he rolled off her and began to dress in a freshly pressed white pair of slacks and a black silk shirt. "On behalf of the

Fourth Reich, I salute you for a job well done," he said as he left.

He examined himself in the mirror and combed his hair, then unlocked the bedroom door and motioned for the two men from the crematorium to enter. "Take her to the oven. She has done her part for the Fourth Reich and The Organization."

Finally, at 1:00 p.m. sharp, one of the SS personnel stopped the music. Everyone's attention turned to the patio entrance and saw Dr. Hausser approach. Applause filled the room. Hausser waited a few seconds before raising his arms, requesting that the applause stop. Jeannie watched.

"Ladies and gentlemen, thank you for coming to my island where history has been repeated in glorious fashion." Several of the females admiringly whispered what fine shape the doctor was in. Others spoke of how lively and youthful he looked. Some speculated about his age, while others wondered if he was married.

He motioned to the SS guards to close all doors exiting the hospital into the patio, and to remove the native girls serving food and refilling champagne glasses. Once satisfied that only authorized individuals were present, he began. "Seventy-six years ago, toward the end of World War II, Adolf Hitler, our Fuhrer, chose to take his own life rather than fall into the hands of the Untermensch. He would not allow filth such as communists and Jews study him before they tortured him to death. No, instead he chose the honorable thing to do. But, in the process, the world lost the greatest leader of all time. Until now."

Some higher ups knew what Dr. Hausser was referring too, many did not. They turned to each other, questioning what Hausser was talking about. He allowed them to talk among themselves as he unwrapped a cigar he had in his breast pocket and lit it. He took a draw and then placed it into the notch of a white ashtray.

Taking a spoon off the table, he hit the side of his half-empty champagne glass to regain everyone's attention. Silence blanketed the room; only the low whine of the hospital's air conditioning units persisted. "Let's get down to business shall we. The leaders of The Organization have devoted many years and enormous effort, plus a large portion of their fortune, to get us where we are today." He paused. "Today that time, effort, sweat and blood culminate in not only the creation of the Fourth Reich, but the destiny of the Aryan race as envisioned by the Fuhrer." Some of the uniformed SS men clicked their heels together and gave the Hitler salute. Others in the room mumbled their thoughts, still trying to decipher Hausser's message.

"This is not an exaggeration my friends, it is literally the truth. One must only watch the news and television shows to see the works of the devilish Jews. They have recruited the Slavs and Semites, the Black, Yellow, and Brown to pollute the Aryan Race, not to mention their acceptance of homosexuality. Over seventy years ago, the Fuhrer and Deputy Reichsfuhrer Hinrich Himmler had a plan to produce more Aryan youth. My great-grandfather, Joseph Mengele, conducted thousands of experiments at Auschwitz in pursuit of that goal. This brings us to the present, ladies and gentlemen."

He picked up his cigar and tapped the ash away. After sipping some of his remaining champagne, he looked at the crowd assembled. "My staff and I have continued my great-grandfather's experiments, but with one new aim in mind. He looked at his head surgical nurse, Frau Becker, and nodded. She turned and left the patio. "Any movement, any new government, must have a strong leader. Someone who is of the Aryan race. Second, they must be able to see the future and instill nationalist pride in his people."

He paused and heard the patio doors open. "Ladies and gentlemen, it sounds like I am describing our beloved Fuhrer, and if fact, I am. I am honored to inform you that we have been successful in cloning our wonderful leader, Adolf Hitler."

Some shouted Heil Hitler and clicked their heels. Most of the women opened their mouths in shock and were lost for words. Others just focused on the open patio doors. The surgical nurse entered the patio pushing an incubator followed by three other nurses also pushing incubators. They were placed in front of the assembled group.

"More precisely, we have been successful in cloning four infants containing the DNA of our Fuhrer." Thunderous applause filled the room intermixed with "Heil Hitler." Dr. Hausser took it all in with a prideful smile. Several from the crowd approached Hausser, wanting to shake his hand. Others approached the four incubators to see the infants.

Two elderly males slowly approached Hausser. When he saw them approach, he quickly came to attention but did not offer the Hitler salute. The older of the two was Claus Meyer, head of The Organization. Rolf Becker would be his successor. Reaching Hausser, Becker shook his hand and offered his congratulations. Meyer did not.

"Herr Doctor," Meyer began. "What is the meaning of creating four clones? What do you expect The Organization to do? Wait for them to grow up and then have gladiator games to see who is the fittest of the four?"

"General Meyer. Let me explain." Before he could begin, he was interrupted by other guests wanting to shake his hand. Meyer turned to them and glared. The procession leading to Hausser dispersed immediately. "Go ahead, Herr Doctor, you were saying," Meyer said with a little distain in his voice.

"General, we used ten Aryan subjects in the cloning process, not knowing for certain how many would make it to full term. It is not like a normal pregnancy. We had to determine when the subjects are fertile and then impregnate them. We must then wait to see if the egg implanted into their fallopian tube takes. It is a painstaking process. We even continued after several were known to be successes."

He wanted to continue, but Meyer raised his right hand and stopped him. "Herr Doctor. We are extremely impressed with the work you have done. You have the medical degree, I do not. But I do know that to successfully clone not one, but four fetuses is remarkable, not only for being able to clone a human, but to embed our Fuhrer's DNA into their chromosomes. For that, again, I salute you. I am simply asking, what are we going to do with four identical infants. There can only be one Adolf Hitler."

Hausser was a little frustrated at having to wait for General Meyer to complete his thoughts, but respectfully waited until he was through.

"Herr General. For several years we will have to watch and evaluate each infant."

"Monitor them for what purpose?" Meyer angrily interrupted.

Swallowing to help keep his composure, Hausser continued. "We must monitor not only their physical health, but also the development of their personality. We will determine which of the four clones exhibits the personality traits closest to our Fuhrer and our political ideology? Once that is determined, the others can be eliminated. The DNA of a person, in this case, our Fuhrer, can only produce an exact duplicate of the human being. Its personality and ideology is something that is learned."

Meyer paused and looked at Becker and then back to Hauser. "I see. I won't ask how long that will take, but I will have to report back to the executive committee, Herr Doctor. But for now, please proceed, and again, congratulations," the General said while he and Becker approached the four incubators.

The surgical nurse, who overheard the discourse between Meyer and Hausser, approached the doctor. "Those ungrateful swine. Do they not know what you've gone through all these years in the recreation of our Fuhrer?"

Hausser raised his hand to stop her from saying anything more. "I am not bitter, Frau. In fact, I knew they would not want to share any glory for our righteous acts. In the end, you and I will be held in the highest esteem over these two louts. Come. Let us now finish the charade."

Once again tapping on his now empty champagne glass, Hausser directed all eyes back to him. "And now, it is time to deliver these magnificent creations to those honored families selected by The Organization to raise our young Fuhrer in National Socialism ideology." Looking around the room he could sense the anticipation of those who had gone through the screening process. Over 100 families had been rigorously scrutinized, and only the "best" families would raise the infants. Meyer and Becker thought there would be only one "Fuhrer."

Now, witnessing four, they realized their odds of being selected had grown.

"The first parents selected by The Organization are Herr Schneider and his wife." Enthusiastic applause accompanied the two as they approached the first incubator. "Please stand by your child until I conclude my presentation so we might take photos of this glorious occasion," Hausser requested, before continuing.

"The second family is Herr Wagner and his beautiful wife." The couple followed the Schneider's example and stood near incubator number two.

"The proud parents of infant number three is Herr Werner and his spouse." More applause.

"And finally, the final family awarded by The Organization entrusted to raise, nurture, and groom our Fuhrer goes to that of Herr Franke and Elsa."

Around 11:00 p.m., many of Hausser's guest began leaving. A little before midnight, Jeannie heard what must have been the last seaplane departing the island and circling overhead. Hausser was relieved after seeing General Meyer and Becker off. He was driven back up to the main house, exhausted from such a long day. Pouring himself a glass of cognac and lighting his second cigar of the day, he sat in his plush leather chair, thinking about the future and what he had already accomplished for the Fourth Reich. The final step would be taken the following day.

The next morning, he slept until almost 10:00. Realizing the noon hour was fast approaching, he skipped taking a shower and proceeded to the hospital. He found the lead surgical nurse in the nursery sitting in a rocking chair, cradling an infant. "How is he doing today?" he asked, startling the nurse.

"Fine, Herr Doctor. He put on a little more weight since you last examined him." She rose, placed the infant back in the incubator and closed the lid. Hausser walked to the incubator and looked at the infant. "Good morning, mein Fuhrer."

"You must make an announcement today to all the staff. They have forty-eight hours to leave the island. I have arranged for seaplanes to start arriving at 10:00 a.m. starting two days from today. They will come every two hours until finally you and I leave with the infant. Tell them to make sure all documents here in the hospital are destroyed."

"But, Herr Doctor, does that include your personal notes?"

"No, I will take care of my documents. Just concentrate on any medical records here."

His thought process was interrupted when his phone rang. Glancing at the screen to see who was calling, he saw "Unknown caller." "Hello," he said hesitantly.

"Herr Doctor. There has been a change in plans. I got word just now that Interpol as well as the American FBI are very close to finding you. You must escape as soon as possible. At most, you have only two days." The call was suddenly terminated before Hausser could ask questions.

"Frau. The authorities are closer than we thought. Tell the staff they must be ready to leave the island tomorrow. They only have twenty-four hours. I will make arrangements for the planes to start arriving at ten in the morning. We must hurry."

Hausser summoned the two men who abducted Jeannie and told them she would be leaving the next morning on the same plane carrying him, Frau Becker and the infant. "Sedate her first thing in the morning and secure her in the plane."

TWENTY-NINE

Delaney walked the long hallway in the Brazilian Interpol office, got a cup of coffee and then took a seat in the breakroom. The coordinates Darcy received pinpointed an area with several uncharted islands off the Argentinian coast. He had spent most of the night talking with his director as well as Lomax. What do the Americans say all the time? Hurry up and wait?" he thought.

"Agent Delaney. There's a priority one phone call for you," a young Brazilian Interpol agent said, pointing in the direction of a separate office. God, I hope this call will lead somewhere, he was thinking as he prepared to take the call.

Delaney received approval from his director to proceed as warranted with the S-Branch now housed near the Buenos Aries airport. He personally would be leading the team, conducting a black ops investigation without the knowledge of the Argentine government, a body usually reluctant to extradite anyone Interpol sought. The less they knew, the better.

At the airport he met members of the S-Branch who were awaiting confirmation as to which island

Jeannie was being held captive. Once that was known, they would prepare their assault. This is where it gets dicey, Delaney thought. He had explained to Lomax that the Interpol and FBI legal departments were attempting to come up with all possible charges against Dr. Hausser. Thus far, they only had Max's confession that incriminated him. Hopefully the raid would net physical evidence, including Jeannie's safe return. Anything related to the kidnapped females and their current location would be helpful.

Hausser supervised the transportation of final staff members leaving the island. He and Frau Becker were the last to leave. The incubator was placed in the seaplane and the two boarded with the infant. Jeannie was sedated and restrained in a rear seat. In case she woke up, Hausser had a Taser in his pocket.

He instructed the pilot to take off and the plane gradually accelerated, bouncing a few times on waves created by a strong wind before it ascended. Hausser took one final look at his island as the plane circled the cove and gained altitude. This had been his home for many years, but now with the experiment completed, he and his lead nurse would be raising young Adolf in Hitler's birthplace, Braunau am Inn in Upper Austria, on the border with Germany.

Under fake names, he and Frau Becker would live as the young child's grandparents, telling that the child's birthparents died in a car accident. Hausser believed this story would not raise suspicion. Once the boy reached thirteen, arrangements would be made to exterminate the other four clones and their appointed guardians. Only he, and he alone, could create the new Fuhrer as a perfect Adolf Hitler replacement. Yes, General Meyer, there can only be one Fuhrer, he thought over and over during the long flight that required many fueling stops in route to Austria.

Delaney and his S-Branch team members were dressed in civilian clothes when they met at the airport. Following introductions, they were escorted to a private hanger by an Interpol agent who predominantly talked to Delaney. A helicopter was fueled and ready within the hanger. Delaney called for one final head call in the hanger and they began their wait.

Delaney received a call from headquarters. The plane appeared have headed toward a group of unnamed islands, and its altitude suggested that one of them had to be its destination, but which one? Delaney called everyone over to a table displaying an overhead view of the islands. The waiting continued.

During the early morning hours while Delaney's second in command, Danny Holt--whom everyone called Danny Boy--was outlining several contingency plans that could be used regardless on which island the plane touched down, Delaney received a second call. Upon concluding it, he interrupted the briefing with the latest intel.

"We're told the plane landed on this island," he said, pointing to a speck on the map. "It has no name. These recent flyover photos show that this side of the island appears uninhabited. What do you think Danny? We approach from the west? Then by cutting through here, we'll have a direct route to this house (pointing) that appears to be the main residence. We're not sure what this structure is (again pointing)." Danny looked at the latest photos. "I think that's the best plan.

"First, we secure this building," pointing to what will later be known as Hausser's residence. "From there we'll assault the larger of the two," pointing to the hospital. "Assume we'll run into armed resistance. Take whatever action is deemed necessary."

"Remember," Delaney added. "Agent Loomis is our primary objective. Her safe release is paramount. Any questions?" None were asked.

The helicopter ride from Buenos Aires took a little under four hours, during which there was little conversation among those on board. Delaney appeared to be lost in thought. The helicopter landed in an open field of what look liked a sugar cane planation. The sun had not yet risen, but everyone could feel the humidity rising. Steam rose from the numerous ferns that dominated the pathway.

Mosquitos viciously greeted the advancing team. Thirty-five minutes later they reached the outside of the compound. By then, there was enough sunlight to clearly see the main house and what appeared to be a hospital. Delaney told the team to take ten so they could regain their breath.

"OK people, listen up," Danny Boy said, and began giving instructions. "You two approach from this side. You provide sniper cover from here. Okay. Let's get this party started."

Delaney and the S-Branch surgically approached the house. The sniper notified the team that no activity was observed. The ground force made it to the residence and found it unlocked. Entering the structure, the three continued to monitor. "All clear, all clear," indicating that thus far the house was empty, was heard on everyone's earpiece.

One S-Branch member was left at the house once it was confirmed that it was unoccupied. The rest of the team followed the team leader through the garden path to the hospital after the sniper re-established a new viewing point. "Team leader. No activity seen here either," he reported as the team advanced. Delaney waited near the house and did not start down the garden path.

"What the hell?" the sniper said.

"Do you have movement?" the team leader asked.

"No. The structure appears to be a hospital, and there's a large Nazi and SS flag mounted over the entrance."

The team leader and two others entered the clearing from the garden path to the hospital and saw the flags described by their sniper. The remaining members advanced from the patio which was also decorated, not only with SS flags and the Nazis emblem, but with a large photo of Adolf Hitler.

The hospital took much longer to secure than Hausser's residence due to its size. Receiving the "all clear," most of the S-Branch began searching the main quarters while Delaney met up with the team leader at the entrance to the hospital. "What the hell was this place used for?" the team leader asked. "Best not to know," Delaney replied. "Looks like they left in a hurry."

No evidentiary items were found in the house, including what was assumed to be Hausser's master bedroom. There were no signs of Jeannie. The agents left the house and walked through the garden to the hospital where the entire S-Branch reassembled. "Guys, you won't believe what you're going to see," Delaney said as he saw them approach. "This was a fully functioning hospital. Well, more of a maternity ward." They followed Delaney into the main hospital, and after passing through a reception area they came upon a nursing station with empty clipboards.

"Looks like someone was in a hurry cleaning up the place," one team member said.

"Looks like it. Still no Jeannie," Delaney replied.

They found a floor with numerous hospital beds and several incubators.

"Look at this," Delaney said, pointing to a fully operational lab which, well devoid of scientists and medical workers and documents, still had a vast array of drugs in the cabinets. Passing an indoor swimming pool and recreation area, they entered an elevator that took them to the basement. There, they saw several hospital beds as well as a huge commercial grade cremation oven. All Delaney could say, looking at the oven, was "Oh my God!"

Delaney opened the oven door and saw human remains among the ash. "Someone did not allow the oven to complete its task. Looks like we have a few skulls in here."

"Well, we can't call for an evidence team to respond, so let's see if we can find some bags and process the scene as best we can," Johnny Boy replied. "I also want to go through the house one more time to make sure we didn't miss anything."

They returned to the elevator and checked the remaining floors, finding nothing useful. Delaney collected the skulls from the basement oven. Someone didn't do a good job of erasing the whiteboard, one of the agents said. He could make out the words, Subject #1, Subject #2, Subject #5, Subject #7 and Subject #10. "What happened to subjects three, four, six, eight and nine?" he wondered. On the floor next to an emptied trash can he found a balled-up piece of paper which he smoothed out on the desk. "Shit!" he said out loud, and searched for Delaney.

He heard the elevator chime announcing its arrival on the first floor. "He cloned five infants. There are five of them!" he told Delaney.

THIRTY

Believing they had obtained all the evidence they could from the residence and hospital, Johnny Boy requested that the helicopter pick them up near a clearing by the boat dock. "Thank God we don't have to go back into that jungle!" one of the team members said. They arrived back at the hanger in Buena Aries where Delaney debriefed the team and then left for the main airport. "Back to the waiting game," Delaney said to no one in general. He called Lomax and provided an update.

"Well, at least we have enough evidence to process," Delaney said. "If the skulls match any of our missing women, we'll know we're on the right track." The team leader nodded at Delaney who was still trying to process the fact that Hausser had cloned five infants carrying Hitler DNA. But where were these infants now? Does Hausser have all of them? And where did they take Jeannie? he wondered. He fought images of Jeannie being brutalized by Hausser.

While waiting for his flight back to San Francisco, Delaney received a call from his supervisor. "Sean, intelligence states there were numerous small aircrafts leaving the island late last night before you raided the compound. The last plane left a few hours before you arrived and appears to be flying toward Western Europe."

With the approval of his supervisor, Delaney rearranged his flight to Berlin. He thought that Hausser and Jeannie had to be on the last flight leaving the island and doubted they would be flying to Great Britain. He arranged to transfer the evidence, including the skulls, to an Interpol agent at the airport for processing before he was in the air.

"Hello, Agent Delaney. This is Darcy. Lomax informed us that neither Jeannie nor the doctor were on the island, so I decided to try something in an attempt to locate them. I tapped into the Buenos Aires airport's security camera footage and database using facial recognition and located Hausser. He wasn't in the main terminal, but in one of the smaller feeder facilities. He's traveling with a late forties to early fifties female and get this, they have an infant with them. I didn't see Jeannie. They probably had her secured in the plane while it was being refueled. The latest flight is being monitored by the CIA. The pilot put the plane on a course to Austria."

"Wow! Someday you have to privately tell me how you get all this information. Okay, here's what I want you to do. It's a long shot, but let's see if we can get lucky for once. Go back thirty-six hours and check for passengers leaving the Buenos Aires airport with a baby."

"A baby?" Darcy asked.

"Yes. I'll explain later. Then I want you to track their flights out of Argentina, and from there I'd like to know their final destination if possible. I know I'm asking a lot but get Burk to help out. Please tell your SAC that this was a request from me. I don't want you two to get into any trouble."

Delaney then called the Berlin Interpol office and was connected with the bureau chief. "Can you get your top researchers to do some urgent work for us? My go-to people are presently tied-up looking at flight manifests and photos. I need someone to do a complete workup on Adolf Hitler's birth. Where was he born? Who were his parents? Where was he raised? What schools did he attend? And so forth, just up until he enters his teenage years. That should be enough."

Feeling he needed to make personal contact with Lomax, Delaney called him. Lomax answered on the second ring. Delaney began, "Sir, you'll probably think I'm crazy. Everything's quite fluid now as you can imagine, but I wanted to review with you what we know about Hausser and his genetic cloning experiment. He and The Organization have gone to great lengths to find almost identical blonde-haired, blue-eyed females. We now know they were used as surrogates to carry fetuses containing Hitler's DNA to full term. You following me so far?"

"Yes, go ahead," Lomax replied.

"Himmler encouraged Dr. Joseph Mengele and other doctors to experiment on Jewish children in Auschwitz in hopes of finding a way to mass-produce white haired, blue eyed children, Hitler's so called 'master race.' Hausser appears to have advanced genetics far beyond other scientists by producing five Hitler clones. It appears that four of the five clones were given to individuals high up in The Organization. Hausser possesses the fifth infant. Is it too much of a stretch to think that Hausser, himself, will try to replicate Hitler's childhood, exposing the young child to experiences, sights and sounds that the original Hitler encountered during his youth?"

Lomax did not immediately reply, obviously processing what Delaney had just told him. "That does make sense, but my question is, why five clones? Is The Organization trying to raise five Adolf Hitlers? And why kidnap Jeannie?"

"Maybe not," said Delaney. "In the hospital we found ten hospital beds in the maternity ward. We believe there are five infants. What if out of the ten, only five infants survived? With a fifty percent survival rate, Hausser may have decided to allow the five to grow and later determine which of the five most represents their dead leader? He knows that although the fetuses will all look alike and appear similar to

Hitler at that stage of his life, his personality must be learned. I feel Hausser will fill his head with Nazi ideology in the process."

"I think you nailed it," Lomax said. "What limited knowledge I have about cloning was from hearing about a woman who paid over sixty-five thousand dollars to clone her dead cat. The result was an identical copy of her feline, but she was sad that the clone shared none of the personality traits of her original pet. Assuming Hausser was able to make a clone of Hitler, he realizes that it will take some time for his personality to form. Hausser or someone from The Organization will have to monitor the clones' development and then select the one most suitable to become the Fourth Reich leader."

"I've already arranged for my flight to be changed from San Francisco to Berlin. I'm facing a sixteen plus hour flight transfer in Madrid, Spain first. My department's doing a workup on Hitler's birth city, the schools he attended, et cetera."

"Sean. You need to change your flight again," Lomax said. "Hitler was born in Braunau am Inn, in Austria, not Germany. And please, find Jeannie."

"Bloody hell! I should've called you first instead of asking the Germany Interpol office to start the investigation. Thank you! Yes, I need to change my flight. I'll let you know when I'm in Austria. I'm sure Jeannie's taking care of herself. She's very tough." The flight to Austria turned out to take as long as the one to Germany. Delaney tried to sleep on the plane but worry about Jeannie's well-being made it difficult. Why did Hausser have her abducted? he wondered.

After a couple of in-air meals, the plane landed in Austria a few minutes ahead of schedule. A driver awaited Delaney's arrival and took him to the Austrian Interpol office, a space about the same size as his office in San Francisco. The office director greeted him with coffee and chocolate filled croissants. Introductions were made with other Interpol staff, followed by a group looking at an aerial map spread out on a large table that showed a section of Braunau am Inn, Hitler childhood haunt.

Pointing to the map, Director Jakob Bauer stated that this section of the city was the birth place of Adolf Hitler. He then pulled a large colored photo out from under the map and placed in on the table. "This is Salzburger Vorstadt 15," Bauer began. "It's Hitler's home as it looked when he was born, and this photo shows how it looks today.

"My office, per your request, conducted research on the earlier years of Hitler. At the time of his birth, the building was a modest guest house where Hitler's parents rented rooms in connection with his father's job as a minor customs official at the nearby Austrian–German border. The Hitlers only lived in the building until Adolf was three years old when his father was transferred to Passa, a city in lower Bavaria, Germany. After World War II, the building was rented by the Austrian Republic, and in 1952 it obtained heritage protection as part of the historic city center. Until 1965 it was the home of the public library, later it became a bank. From 1970 to 1976, several classes from the technical high school were held in the house, until the school was rebuilt. For many years the house accommodated a charity branch that operated it as a day center and workshops for people with learning difficulties.

"After the charity vacated the building in 2011, it remained empty for several years. In 2016, the Austrian government decided to expropriate the owner and to demolish the building, however a special expropriation law was adopted. It was suggested that since it was Hitler's birthplace, it should become a place of remembrance for victims of Nazism, a thought that had circulated during the early post-war years.

"For a long time, the council discussed the wisdom of marking the house with an attached memorial tablet. Finally, in 1983 a decision was made to place a memorial tablet near the building. I say near, since the owner, who had no connection to Hitler, felt it would be an intrusion on her rights of ownership having it placed on her property. She also feared unwelcomed attention or attacks from anti or Neo-Nazis.

"While you were in the air, my agents did some checking and found that very recently a person looking very much like the photo of Dr. Hausser, a woman with a baby, and a blonde female moved into that address. We believe the blond female is your missing FBI agent Loomis." Delaney felt his heart race.

The Interpol director pointed to a small cottage very close to Hitler's birth home. "My agents are located in this cottage across from Salzburger Vorstadt 15 and it has remained under continuous surveillance. My men have only seen the doctor leave and return once, carrying groceries. It appears that counting the infant, there are only four people inside."

THIRTY-ONE

At some point during the long flight from Haussers' island to Austria, Jeannie believed they had given her something in either her food or drink that knocked her out. She briefly recalled being pushed in a wheelchair. Hausser showed her his Taser and told her to sit on the bed in what appeared to be a small cottage. He withdrew plastic cuffs and told Jeannie to turn around. She turned on the mattress as Hausser requested. He did not seem to notice Jeannie straining her wrists before he applied the cuffs, hoping there would be enough space left for her to work her hands free.

At 7:00 a.m., Delaney, several heavily armed police officers, a few Interpol agents, and an attractive female agent, Amy Fischer, met in the briefing room. Pointing at the cottage, Delaney addressed the officers and agents present.

"Agent Fischer and I will knock on the door. Once the front door opens, we will push our way inside and secure the premises. If shots ring out, bring in the cavalry. Do not shoot the blond woman. She is the hostage."

An Interpol agent dropped off Delaney and agent Fischer a block away from the cottage. Delaney immediately noticed the structure on his right as Hitler's home, and off to the side the plaque they talked about the day before that identified the site. The two began walking up the street holding hands.

Upon reaching the door, Delaney looked at Fischer and, in a whisper, asked if she were ready. She nodded and he knocked on the door. Each held their handgun behind their back. Frau Becker answered the door, but before she could inquire what they wanted, Delaney pushed her aside and Fischer took control of Becker, showing her the weapon she was holding.

Hausser came out from a back bedroom singing a tune and carrying a baby. Seeing Delaney and Fischer, he shouted, "What is the meaning of this?" as he hastily placed the infant in a bassinet near the wall of the hallway leading to the room holding Jeannie.

Delaney began to identify himself, but before he could finish, Hausser pulled a

Walther P38 he had concealed under the baby and pointed it at both Delaney and Fischer, catching them off guard. The infant began to cry. Jeannie heard the commotion, and successfully slipped out of the plastic cuffs and entered the room, drawing the attention of Frau Becker and Hausser. "Stay where you are Agent Loomis," Hausser said.

"Who are you? Are you Jews hunting Nazis?" Hausser asked before breaking into a sinister laugh.

"Are you here to arrest us? You two do not comprehend the historical event that is about to take place. Do you know who this is?" looking at the infant. "This is the second coming of the greatest leader the world has ever known. How did you find us? Is this a plan to rescue your Agent Loomis?"

The nurse placed her hand over her mouth. Jeannie thought she might be trying to suppress a scream. Within seconds the nurse began chocking and foam began forming in her mouth, dripping from her hands onto her dress. Beginning to shake, she suddenly fell to the floor. As Jeannie stooped down to check on her, Hausser fired, striking Jeanne in the shoulder.

Delaney immediately returned fire, hitting Hausser in the upper arm. Turning, Hausser fired another shot toward Jeannie, but the bullet went wide and hit the bassinet. He turned toward Delaney who quickly fired two shots, one to Hausser's chest and the other to his forehead. Becker fired off one round, but it missed wide right, piercing the wall. Dropping his gun, Hausser fell like a rock, the wall behind him sprayed with blood and brain matter.

Seeing that the doctor's gun had fallen away from his body, Delaney checked on Jeannie. Applying pressure to her wound to minimize blood loss, she told him she was fine, Fischer, pointing her gun at Hausser, walked over and kicked his gun even farther away, then bent down to check his pulse. There was none. Then she went to the bassinet to check on the baby and was shocked to see that the baby had a hole in its side and the blanket was becoming saturated with blood. She checked for a pulse but found none there either.

"You gave me a bloody fright going missing like that," Delaney said.

"I love it when you say bloody. Can we go home now?"

Numerous uniformed officers entered the cottage. "Get paramedics in here quickly," Delaney shouted to no officer in particular.

Jeannie assured him that she just received a flesh wound and would be fine. "It bloody hurts, but I'll be OK."

"That's one of the worst pronunciation of 'bloody' I've ever heard. You and Burk need to take a class on how to speak proper British English," Delaney said as he helped Jeannie leave the cottage and enter the care of paramedics who had arrived on the scene.

They stayed in Austria another day, giving Jeannie time to recover while providing the prosecutor's office with all the details of the Hausser investigation. They did not disclose information about The Organization. During the search of the cottage, Delaney found a thumb drive belonging to Hausser and placed it in his pocket for later examination. They were fortunate in finding a direct flight back to San Francisco, and this time they got seats next to each other, holding hands for the first time. Jeannie gave him one of her pain pills. It had enough narcotic in it to give him a well-earned sleep during the flight, sleeping through two of the three meals that were served.

At that juncture they had no information from the cottage search that revealed the whereabouts of the other four infants.

Eighteen and a half hours later they arrived back in San Francisco. Delaney kissed Jeannie's cheek while in the terminal before Ismail and Lomax came to greet them. He told her goodnight and that he would call her in the morning to see how she was feeling.

Unfortunately, Ismail saw the kiss. "Ah ha!" he said when he got Jeannie alone. "Enquiring minds are getting more and more information," he said. Lomax, overhearing the conversation looked confused, having no idea what Ismail was referring to. Jeannie was too tired to banter, and just told Ismail and Lomax to drive her back to the bureau. She would fill them in on the details of Hausser's demise on the way. When they arrived at the bureau, Lomax would not allow her to enter. Instead, he gave her orders to go home and take a few days off, if not more. She did not object and found herself heading down Highway 101 South for the Dumbarton Bridge.

She could not remember the last time she ate, since she also slept through several food calls on the plane. She did a quick inventory in her head about what she had in her kitchen cupboard, but nothing sounded appealing. She stopped at a Carl's Junior and bought a burger, fries and Diet Dr. Pepper. "The hell with the calories," she said to herself. "I'm beat!"

By the time she got into her house it was almost 11:00 p.m. She placed her purse and service weapon on her kitchen counter and took her food into the dining room. "Miss me guys?" she asked her koi as she sprinkled food pellets into the tank and returned to her meal. She turned on the television, but the news made no mention of their investigation. She doubted it would ever be shared. Finishing her dinner, she decided to send emails to Delaney and Ismail saying she would not be in the office the next morning. Instead, she planned on sleeping the night and day away. She sent a long email to Lomax instead of a brief text message, bringing him up to speed about possible loose ends in the case. She told him about her plan to catch up on her sleep, but for him to call if anything urgent happened. She knew he would not call unless it was absolutely necessary.

About ready to climb into bed after taking a hot shower, she remembered asking Delores to come in and care of her fish during her short absence. She taped a note on her front door informing Delores she was home, but in desperate need of sleep and that she had already taken care of the koi. "I will give you all the details once I recover from jet lag," she added to the note.

THIRTY-TWO

As exhausted as she was, she took one last look at her guest bedroom wall displaying pictures of Dr. Hausser and the nurse. Her last thoughts before she fell asleep was the unknown location of the remaining four clones, and of course, Sean.

When Jeannie awakened it took her a little while to comprehend whether it was 3:00 a.m. or 3:00 p.m. "Damned jet lag!" she said, throwing off the tangled blanket and sheet. Looking out her blacked-out windows, she realized that night had given way to early morning. She silently crept through her house, hoping that Delores was not outside her front door looking for an indication she was up and about. She made oatmeal and sprinkled cinnamon on it like her mom used to do when she was a child, then toasted two slices of whole wheat bread. Still hungry, she made French toast and cooked two links of pork sausage, washing it all down with a third cup of coffee.

She heard tapping on her kitchen window facing the front yard. "Damn, it must be Delores," she said to herself, and sure enough, it was. "Good morning sunshine. Gee, you get up early," she said, opening the door.

"Oh yeah, Walter and I are early birds. You know that old saying, the early bird catches the worm. Anyway, I wanted to give you a heads-up. Yesterday afternoon, I saw a suspicious man at your front door. I told him you weren't home and asked him if I could help. He was carrying a briefcase, but now days, you never know."

Jeannie could only imagine how this must have played out between Delores and the "suspicious" person. I wonder if she was packing? Jeannie thought, suppressing a smile.

"Anyway, he told me he was an attorney and was trying to reach you. After I told him you weren't home, he wanted to know when you might be returning. I told Walter later that maybe he was trying to case-out your house. You know, how burglars do before they break in? He reached into his jacket pocket and pulled out this card." She handed the card to Jeannie who saw, Richard Jamison, Attorney at Law, with a phone number and address in Fremont, California.

"Huh. Did he say what it was about?" Jeannie asked.

"I asked him, but he said it was confidential. I think he might be a mafia member. He was wearing this really expensive suit and drove a black Porsche. I took his card and said I would give it to you when you came home. He said thank you, and I watched him walk back to his sportscar. I started walking back to my house, turning to make sure he didn't double back on me, and my damned gun fell out of my sweatpants. It didn't get scratched, but I ran home and asked Walter to check it out to make sure I didn't break it."

Jeannie thanked Delores, closed the door and walked back into the kitchen while looking at the card again. A huge smile broke out on her face, thinking about the poor lawyer and the thoughts that must have raced through his mind when he ran into Delores. She placed the business card on the kitchen counter, thinking it was probably someone who wanted to serve her with a subpoena. She would not call him since the standard operating procedure was to drop off subpoenas at the bureau. The legal department would then contact the appropriate agent.

She called Sean to say good morning and to hear his voice. They flirted with each other for over an hour. He, too, had decided to take a few extra days off before heading back to the office. "How's the shoulder?" he asked.

"It's fine. Like I said, it was just a flesh wound. It itches like hell though. I get the stitches out next week." She told him she would make an appearance at the bureau the next morning and asked if he had looked at the thumb drive yet.

"It's heavily encrypted," he replied.

"Why don't you bring it over to the bureau tomorrow and I'll get Darcy and Burk to work on it. They love the challenge of breaking encryptions."

Then she broached a subject that made her heart skip a beat and a little nervous. “Hey, I have a few weeks of comp time built up and I really need to get up to my cabin and check it out. It’s up at Coeur D’ Alene Lake, you know, up in Idaho. I was wondering if you might want to take a little vacation with me up there.”

“Say no more. I’m bloody happy that you asked. I definitely want to go. Just say when and I’ll be there.” Jeannie laughed at his use of “bloody,” and was more than delighted that he wanted to join her. They both knew what that would lead to.

Her next call was to Ismail. His wife answered the phone and pretty much gave Jeannie all the information she wanted about her partner. “Here he is,” she said while passing the phone to him.

“Hey boss. How did you sleep?”

“Well, I must have passed out since I don’t remember any dreams. Before you ask, the shoulder is fine. What about you?” she inquired.

“Glad you asked. I had the weirdest dream. You were one of the Bond girls, and of course, Delaney was double-o-seven. We were tracking down a nefarious doctor, but instead of it being Hausser, it was Dr. No. Remember him from the movies?” Ismail asked. Not waiting for an answer, he continued. “Anyway, we tracked the doctor down to a lab, but then Sean ran into the nurse in my dream, she clicked her shoes together and a knife popped out that had poison on it.”

"I think that's from the James Bond film, From Russia With Love," Jeannie said. "I think her name was Rosa Klebb and she worked for SPECTRE."

"Whatever," Ismail said, "Anyway, I come into the room and see that Sean is in deep shit, so I pull out my gun and shoot her, saving his life. What do you think that means? You're the one with the Ph.D. in psychology.

"I think it means you still haven't seen our resident shrink to treat your ideals of grandeur. You really need help," Jeannie retorted.

"Very funny. So, what's the game plan for tomorrow?" Ismail asked. "Are you planning to come in?"

"Yeah. I want to hear what Burk and Darcy have learned about the remaining four clones, and I want them to start working on Hausser's encrypted thumb drive. Sean will be bringing it over."

"How are they going to track down the other babies when we don't know their names?" Ismail asked.

"Sean asked them to go back thirty-six hours from the time he hit the island with the Interpol team and to look at all footage from security and ticket counter interactions. He wants to see how many people traveled out of Buenos Aires carrying a child. That's how they found out that Hausser also had an infant," Jeannie explained.

"Sounds like a long shot, but you've been on a roll lately. What do you want me to do?" he asked.

"Why don't you finish your favorite spider case. I know you can hardly wait to get back on it, even though its beneath you, given your talent and training."

"Yeah, my favorite case alright! By the way, while you and Mr. Bond were galivanting around Europe, I was putting on the miles driving down to Foster City and the San Mateo County's Sheriff's Department. You might can call me the 'Travelin Man.' You know, that old Ricky Nelson song." On cue, he began singing:

"'I'm a travelin' man
I've made a lot of stops
All over the world
And in every part I own the heart
Of at least one lovely girl"

Before he could begin the second verse, Jeannie shouted into the phone, "See you tomorrow!" and hung up.

Bright and early the next day, Jeannie was driving over the Dumbarton bridge into the city by the bay. The traffic was heavy, but Jeannie didn't care. She noticed the Cow Palace exit and remembered the shootout there with the jihadists, then passed the old turnoff for Candlestick Park and recalled again attending baseball and football games with her mom and dad. In a good mood, she stopped and picked up fresh bagels and cream cheese before arriving at the bureau.

"Hi, Jeannie. I heard you got to go to Vienna," her secretary said as Jeannie was picking up her "While-U-Where-Out" forms to take to her office.

"Yes, but I was so tired by then that I can't really tell you anything about the city. I'll have to return some day. Any of these urgent?" she asked while glancing at her phone messages.

"Not really. They can all wait," her secretary answered.

Handing a bagel, small container of cream cheese and spoon to her secretary, Jeannie headed to the breakroom. SAC Lomax was already seated with a cup of coffee. He spied the bagels and cream cheese and told Jeannie to just lay them on the table where he was sitting. "So, what's left of your Nazi case?" Jeannie knew he really didn't care, being more interested in putting cream cheese on his bagel. She gave him an update anyway.

Lomax left following the update, leaving Jeannie alone in the breakroom where she was soon joined by Ismail, Burk and Darcy. "You guys did a great job of tracking down Hausser. Agent Delaney will be here sometime this morning with Hausser's thumb drive. Interpol was unsuccessful in getting past the encryption, so I told them I have two of the best in the business who would love to give it a shot."

"Great," said Darcy. "We have more news for you, however." We have now identified three of the four couples that have a clone and their last known residences." Burk handed Jeannie a list of names:

Herr Schneider – Berlin
Herr Wagner – Berchtesgaden, in the Alps
Herr Werner – Obersalzberg, near Eagle's Nest

"When we showed this list to the SAC, he said these were all Hitler's favorite places," Darcy said, taking a bagel. "I've already shared this information with Interpol."

"I wonder what will happen to them and those infants?" Burk asked to no one in particular.

"Well, if this were to take place in the US, you'd be talking about one hell of a jurisdiction nightmare. I'm sure the infants would be placed in shelter care and maybe farmed out to foster homes. After that, who knows," Ismail stated.

"Gee, foster care. But I guess that would be better than being raised by a bunch of Nazis," Jeannie added.

"But what about clone five, depending on which one you assigned to Hausser. There's still one clone out there," Darcy said. No one had an answer.

Delaney arrived around 10:00 a.m. Walking down the hallway, he ran into Lomax who had just used the rest room. "Thanks for getting Jeannie back safely," Lomax said as soon as he saw Sean. "Also, mums the word about your special branch. I was very impressed with their abilities."

"Thank you, sir. Is Jeannie in her office? I have Hausser's encrypted thumb drive and I can't wait to see what's on it."

"She might still be in the breakroom with Ismail, Burk and Darcy. I'd check there first. Again, hell-of-a-job!"

Delaney joined the group still in the breakroom. Darcy was sharing the names of corporations connected to The Organization, and how many she will stop patronizing them in the future. She was the first to see Delaney and extended a greeting. He waved his hand to the group as Ismail offered him a bagel and coffee. Jeannie caught herself blushing for no reason and knew that Ismail noticed.

"I believe you have something for me and Burk," Darcy said to Delaney.

"Oh, yes. Here you go. Good hunting," Delaney said. "By the way, Interpol is currently conducting twenty-four seven surveillance on the three residences you two found for us. Not knowing if there are any Organization members on the Austrian or German police departments, we're conducting the investigation solo. Frankly, the hierarchy of Interpol is unsure what steps to take next, but as you Yanks say, its above my pay grade." Everyone laughed.

THIRTY-THREE

As Jeannie and the SAC were going over her Zero-Based-Budget report, she was thinking in the back of her mind about the upcoming romantic trip to Idaho with Sean, but also about why she had not received a subpoena from legal. While the two took a bathroom and coffee break, she squeezed in time to call legal. They had not received any subpoenas for her nor any messages from a Richard Jamison, the attorney who left his card with Delores. Huh! That's strange, she thought.

Jeannie added a few items and submitted her ZBB report to Lomax, telling him she could not have done it without him--which was a joke at this point, since he had already completed the majority of entries. Upon returning to her office, she took out the attorney's business card and gave him a call.

It was answered on the second ring by a female. "Jamison and Bradly."

"Hello, this is Special Agent Jeannie Loomis with the FBI. My neighbor was given a business card from a Mr. Jamison who requested that I give him a call. If this is about serving me with a subpoena, there is a process that must be followed here at the bureau."

"I'm sorry, I don't know why Mr. Jamison would be trying to reach you. He's in his office. Can I transfer you?"

"Yes, please do," Jeannie answered.

"Richard Jamison. Can I help you?" he asked.

"Yes, Mr. Jamison. This is Special Agent Jeannie Loomis. My neighbor said you came to my residence wishing to see me, and as I told your receptionist, if you desire to subpoena me, the paperwork has to be delivered to our legal department who actually does the serving."

"Oh, I'm so sorry for the misunderstanding. No, I don't have a subpoena for you Agent Loomis. I work probate cases here in Alameda County. A colleague from South Carolina asked me to see if I could track you down regarding an estate case they are trying to settle. By the way, your neighbor nearly gave me a heart attack. Are you aware she carries a concealed weapon? When I was walking back to my car, her gun fell to the sidewalk."

Jeannie smiled and decided to have some fun. "Yes, I'm aware she carries it, but she's an excellent shot. In fact, the last time she shot someone, she placed five in the X-ring." Of course, she was referring to the paper "assailant," but she could not resist hearing what type of reaction she would receive from Jamison.

There was a pause on the line for almost five seconds. Jeannie finally broke the silence. "Please, call me Jeannie. Estate case? I don't understand. My parents have been deceased for many years. Whose estate are you handling?"

"Ms. Loomis, can you hang on one minute while I get the file?"

"Please, again, call me Jeannie. And yes, I will hold."

A few seconds later Jamison was back on the line. "Here it is. Frankly, I'm a little nervous. I've never spoken to an actual FBI agent before." Without waiting for a response, he said, "I'm sorry to inform you that your aunt, Sylvia Kincaid, passed away several weeks ago. You have my condolences. You are the only beneficiary listed in her will and trust. Her maiden name was Nelson. Her estate attorney, Gilbert Goldstein, is hoping that perhaps I can review the trust with you in attendance here in our county, thus eliminating the need for either you or a representative from his firm to travel across the US."

"Sylvia Nelson Kincaid? My aunt? I don't understand. Nelson was my mom's maiden name, but I don't know a Sylvia Kincaid, nor did I have an Aunt Sylvia Nelson. Sorry, I don't know anyone by those names. How is she related to me or my family again?"

Jeannie had several aunts and uncles on her father's side, but her mother was an only child, so there were no aunts and uncles from the Nelson side of the family. In fact, Jeannie only had one living aunt left, and she suddenly realized during the conversation that she had not visited her since Christmas two years earlier.

Jamison said, "I'm reviewing the file, which is quite extensive. Perhaps we can schedule an appointment at my office and we can go over the particulars. I'd hate to run into your neighbor again." Jeannie agreed to make the short drive to his Thornton Avenue office and meet with him at 1:00 p.m. that afternoon. This would give Jeannie enough time to pack for her trip north with Sean and arrange for Delores to care for her koi.

Dressed in semi-business attire, Jeannie arrived at Jamison's office at 12:55. There was no receptionist up front. She was probably still out for lunch, Jeannie thought. When she opened the door, a soft chime went off announcing her presence. An older gentleman approached from the hallway. "Ms. Loomis, I'm Richard Jamison."

"Please, call me Jeannie."

Please, " Jamison said, motioning her to his office. Jeannie was impressed. His cherry wood desk had a glass covered inlaid green leather top with several family photos slid beneath the glazing, and was twice the size of hers at the bureau. Behind the desk there were more photos of various family members as well as awards he had received for teaching probate law at several colleges and universities.

A thick file laid open on the right side of the desk. Jeannie could see a picture of an elderly female, but since it was upside down from where she sat, she could not fully bring it into focus. Jamison removed the paperclip holding the picture and handed it to her. "This is your aunt, Sylvia Nelson Kincaid."

Jeannie studied the photo but did not recognize the individual. The woman had silver hair and looked aristocratic. "No, I'm sorry. There must be a mistake. I've never seen this woman." The chime in the other office rang and she heard someone moving a desk chair and then sitting. Jeannie thought it must be his receptionist.

"After our conversation on the phone, I contacted Mr. Goldstein and told him you didn't know of an aunt named Sylvia Nelson Kincaid. He gave me your aunt's background and her estate information. I'm sorry, but before I can continue, do you have any identification with you? A photo ID would be perfect. I don't have to tell you about how the law works, do I?"

Jeannie pulled out her FBI badge and identification, which more than satisfied Jamison. "Great, thank you. That's very impressive." While Jeannie put her identification back in her purse, Jamison pulled out a legal sized yellow note pad with a large number of bulleted items and began to summarize the notes.

"Sylvia Nelson Kincaid died at the age of nine-seven. She was married for over forty years to a Steven Kincaid. They had no children. She was born and died in Myrtle Beach, South Carolina which is in Horry County, outliving her husband by almost thirty years. She never re-married."

"Sorry, Mr. Jamison, but like I said, I don't know this woman nor did my mom have any siblings," Jeannie replied.

"Let me continue and I think you'll get a better picture. Your mother did in fact have a sister, Sylvia (pointing to the picture). Sylvia was eight years older. I believe your mother was born in Myrtle Beach, South Carolina correct?"

"Well, yes. She was born and raised there, but after she met and married my father, she moved to California."

"Your father fought in the Korean war?" Jamison asked.

"Yes, he did. How did you know that?"

"Okay. According to Mr. Goldstein, your mother and her sister were very much in love with another soldier, a Mr. Paul Radcliff. Mr. Radcliff loved the attention he was receiving from both your mom and her sister. Radcliff enlisted in the Air Force and was later shot down and killed. Something happened between your mom and her sister after his death, and they never spoke to each other again. For what reason? I'm afraid Mr. Goldstein doesn't know the answer to that question.

"Your aunt married Steven Kincaid sometime later. He inherited a coal mining firm from his parents, a large mining firm I might add. Your aunt was quite the businesswoman, and with her help the firm grew progressively larger. After his death and when she was eighty-seven years old, she began suffering a series of strokes that eventually caused her death. She sold her shares of stock in the mining company, and subsequently sold the company to a mining conglomerate.

"In her trust are instructions about what to do with her body, which was buried in a cemetery in Myrtle Beach near her husband. She listed you as her only beneficiary, besides her cat. In other words, you inherit everything, including the care of her feline. If you agree, I can have you complete the forms necessary for me to act as an agent for the Goldstein firm, and we can proceed to the reading of the will and trust and wrap the matter up."

"Wait. I'm sorry. This all comes as a shock," Jeannie admitted. "All my life I understood that my mother was an only child. Her parents died when I was an infant in a car accident, so I never got to meet them. But I've seen pictures of them and my mom, but I never saw pictures of my mom with a sister."

"I wish I could give you more answers Jeannie, but Mr. Goldstein said he doesn't have that information. Some event must have occurred that caused your grandparents to disavow the existence of your mom's sister, your aunt. Other than a birth certificate that Mr. Goldstein obtained, there's little to go by. There's a safe deposit box at a bank in Myrtle Beach, and Mr. Goldstein said he has your aunt's key that he'll arrange for you to pick it up. Perhaps there are contents in the box that might shed light on your questions. This might be a great investigation for you someday, being that you're an FBI agent. Would you like to proceed with me acting as Mr. Goldstein's representative?"

Agreeing that Jamison could act as her aunt's estate attorney Goldstein's representative, in addition to looking out for her, Jeannie signed several forms which Jamison's receptionist immediately faxed back to Goldstein's firm. A short time later, Jamison received a phone call from Goldstein who requested to talk with Jeannie. On speakerphone she confirmed her desire to have Jamison take over the proceedings and thanked him.

"Well, now that we've got that out of the way, let's proceed. Jeannie, your aunt was an extremely wealthy woman, and I need to stress the word 'extremely.' She and your uncle--her husband--amassed a tremendous amount of wealth, both while they were married and through financial decisions your aunt made after his passing.

"One oh her residences alone, a beach front condo which is now yours, is valued about approximately $700,000 dollars and has no mortgage." Jeannie was in shock and barely heard the rest of the estate information Jamison was revealing. Her main residence on Ocean Boulevard is valued at over $ 3 million dollars.

"With the residences and profits from stocks and other assets, Jeannie, in total you will be inheriting over $8 million dollars."

THIRTY-FOUR

SS Captain Franke's wife, Gerta, was strolling with her husband and their infant around the upper deck of the cruise ship. "I am so glad you decided to take our time returning home from Hausser's island by taking a cruise. I think this is wunderbar and he really seems to like it," she said, bouncing the infant in her arms. She looked at her assigned clone and commented on his blue eyes. Frank brushed the small amount of hair on the infant's head. "Here is the future of the Aryan Race. Our new Fuhrer."

Ismail decided to take Burk with him to visit the last two labs on their list. He had put it off long enough and wanted to wrap it up before Jeannie gave him any guff. The next morning after a brief meeting with Jeannie, Ismail and Burk set out to meet Ronald who never called, per Ismail's request. "Here we go. Two highly trained FBI agents and what are we investigating? A bunch of damned spiders," Ismail said, not expecting a reply from Burk. I knew when I left my business card that this asshole would never call."

"Thanks for asking me to come along. It's nice to get out of the computer lab every once in a while. So, who are we going after?" Burk asked. Ismail filled him in while they drove to the lab located in the industrial area near the Oakland estuary.

Ronald Hastings lived in the warehouse district near the Oakland shoreline. Ismail told Burke that the area was now called Middle Harbor Shoreline Park. It encompassed San Francisco Bay and the Port of Oakland entrance channel west of downtown Oakland and was owned and operated by the Port of Oakland. The park entrance was at the intersection of 7th Street and Middle Harbor Road. A quick Google check found that the area was open seven days a week from 8:00 a.m. to dusk.

While they were driving to the listed address, Burk requested a wants and warrant check which came back negative. His residence was a rundown warehouse set off by itself near the water's edge. They saw lights emanating from the second floor windows, but after they rang the doorbell, the lights went out. They waited, thinking that whoever was upstairs might be making their way down to the door. After several minutes, they realized it was not going to happen.

Ismail called the phone number taken from Ronald's employment records at the lab, but it went to voice mail. "Do you smell that?" Ismail asked Burk. "Yeah, it smells like sewer waste," Burk replied.

"No, that smell is reminiscent of each of the labs. It's coming from either a bunch of dead crickets or rat droppings. This guy has a lab here. You know, it could also be the smell of a corpse, don't you think" Ismail asked and winked at Burk.

"Sounds like probable cause to me," Burk said while Ismail tried the door and found it open after a good kick. The odor was extremely pungent. The room was so dark that Burk and Ismail had to pull out their pen lights in order to check the downstairs. There were many empty cages, similar to the those used in two of the labs for macaws, but there were no birds. They both heard a cough upstairs and focused their lights on the staircase. Ismail was in the lead and reached a closed door.

"FBI. Come out and show your hands!" Ismail shouted. No response. "This is the FBI. Come out and show your hands!" Ismail yelled once more. He tried the door, and finding it unlocked like the other, he slowly opened it while standing to the side. The door suddenly opened from the other side and someone grabbed his arm and yanked him into the room, throwing him off balance. He crashed into something made of glass and felt a shard cut his upper left arm as he fell to the floor, his gun sliding out of reach into the darkness. As Burk entered, he was hit on the head and fell to the ground unconscious. Ismail was picked up from the floor and again thrown into several glass containers that crashed at his feet. He was finally able to grab hold of his assailant's clothing and kicked him in the groin. A grunt came from his attacker and Ismail followed the sound. The suspect quickly recovered and punched Ismail in the face, knocking him to the floor once again. Ismail touched his face and felt two spiders crawling on it, followed by two stings, and then tingling in his lips. He knew he had been bitten.

The suspect opened the door and tried to escape, but as he turned away to descend the stairs, Ismail kicked him in the back, causing the culprit to fall forward down the stairs face-first, landing on the first floor either knocked out cold or dead. Ismail could care less. He felt two more bites on his hand and several on his leg under his pants as he bent down to see how badly Burk was injured. Having lost his flashlight in the scuffle, he pulled out his cell and used it to illuminate the room. He grabbed and began shaking Burk in a successful effort to revive him. Burk came-to and shook his head to reorientate himself. Ismail found Burk's flashlight nearby, and after a few shakes, got it to come on. The floor seemed to be moving, and as he cleared his head, he realized that hundreds of spiders were crawling all over it, and the walls that were now visible were lined with over 30 aquariums, not counting the ones he broke while fighting his assailant. Attempts to brush several spiders off Burk's pants, led to more bites on his hand. Ismail got Burk to his feet, squishing spiders under their shoes, and the two headed for the exit, slamming the door behind them. Within minutes, Ismail felt his heart racing as he began to sweat, become nauseous, and began to vomit.

Ismail and Burk had to step over Ronald who was lying at the bottom on the stairs. Burk checked for a pulse, and finding a strong one, cuffed the assailant and rushed to their car where Ismail was having trouble breathing. Burk called dispatch, requesting an ambulance and explaining that they had been envenomated by several Sydney Funnel Web spiders. He also requested that someone in animal control be sent but warned that they would be dealing with very venomous spiders--hundreds of them.

THIRTY-FIVE

Jeannie and Delaney met Darcy in the hospital cafeteria. Both Ismail and Burk had received numerous spider bites, with Ismail receiving the most. They went to Burk's room first. Delaney was holding on to balloons and carrying two presents, one for Burk and the other for Ismail. When the two entered Burk's room, they found him sitting up with two large red circles on his swollen forehead.

"I've heard a lot of excuses to get out of work, but this takes the cake," Jeannie said. "How do you feel?"

"Fine, except around the bite areas. Those little bastards are nasty. They might let me out tomorrow, but I heard from the nurse that Ismail might have to stay at least another day."

"That's what we heard from his wife last night," Jeannie said. "Do you need anything?"

"No. I have Darcy to care for me." Jeannie noticed Darcy blush. Their relationship was the worst kept secret in the bureau. "Here's a snack that should aid in your recovery," Delaney said, handing him one of two boxes he had been carrying. As Burk opened it, Jeannie tied a balloon to the foot of Burk's bed. He did not notice the Spiderman design. “Wow! Sheri’s Berries. Thanks, guys. These are so good.”

“You take care of yourself. I’ll definitely stop by in the future to see how you’re doing, but don’t overdue yourself,” Delaney said, patting Burk on a leg and causing him to jump. “Sorry about that, mate!”

Darcy remained with Burk while Delaney and Jeannie went to Ismail’s room. Ismail’s oldest daughter came out, saw Jeannie and ran up to her. “Jeannie, my dad’s in here,” she said. Jeannie could not remember her name, but Ismail’s daughter grabbed her arm and took her to the room. Delaney trailed them, still holding on to four large helium-filled balloons with Spiderman on the front, as well as a wrapped package.

“Hey Ace. How are you doing?” Jeannie asked while giving his wife a kiss on the cheek.

“How am I doing? I nearly got killed by a bunch of blood-thirsty spiders,” he said, and then turned his attention to Delaney and the balloons.

“Very funny! Very funny! Spiderman. Here I’m on my death bed and my boss has her boyfriend come in with Spiderman balloons.” With that, it was time for Jeannie to blush. “Do you see the type of harassment I put up with from the boss lady here?” Ismail asked his wife, who was looking at Jeannie while laughing and shaking her head.

“How do you put up with him?” Jeannie asked.

Delaney ignored the boyfriend reference. He asked Ismail how he was feeling and handed the wrapped box to Jeannie. When Jeannie placed in on Ismail chest, he reacted as if it caused intense pain. "You weren't bitten on the chest, Izzy," his wife said.

"Oh, I wasn't? Must be my brain overreacting to the life and death struggles I endure for the FBI. What's in the box? If it's a bunch of spiders, even pretend spiders, you two won't see your next birthdays."

"You know. Threatening a federal agent is a felony, even in this wacko state. Just open the box," Jeannie said.

He removed the wrapping paper, taking note of the Spiderman theme and then found a Styrofoam box. "What is this? Honey, maybe you should open it," he said to his wife.

"Just open it," she replied, shaking her head and admitting her husband was an idiot.

He pried the box lid open and found cool packs. Removing them, he found numerous links of Portuguese linguica, morcela (blood sausage), and hot links. "Now we're talking," Ismail said. This is the kind of food needed for a speedy recovery."

"Hey, I heard you're probably getting out of here day after tomorrow. The SAC doesn't want to see you until next week." Addressing Ismail's wife, Jeannie continued. "Unfortunately, you'll have to put up with him since I'm leaving for Idaho for a week."

"Idaho. Wow!" Ismail exclaimed. Jeannie could tell he really wanted to add an insinuation to his comment, but with Delaney in the room he only smiled and went back to examining his goodie box.

"Yeah, the SAC said he can handle the ship until you and I return, so why not get out of Dodge for a little while. Okay, you probably need to get some rest. I'll give you a call once I get to the cabin." She gave Ismail a kiss on his forehead and one on his wife's cheek again. Delaney shook both their hands and they left.

As Jeannie turned the corner, she put up her hand, motioning for Sean to wait a minute, and then put her finger across her lips, indicating for him to be quiet.

"Izzy. Who was that attractive man with Jeannie? No one introduced us. I think there's something going on between the two," Ismail's wife said.

"You don't recognize James Bond, Mr. Double-O-Seven?" he replied.

"What do you mean, James Bond. That's not Sean Connery."

"Well, his first name is Sean."

Jeannie smiled as she and Sean headed to the parking lot, knowing that when they returned to the bureau, Ismail would be throwing a lot of questions her way. At the moment, instead of entertaining romantic thoughts of Sean and her at the cabin, she could not grasp the reality of being a multi-millionaire. Her mom used to talk about Myrtle Beach, how it was like Santa Cruz, California on steroids, but they never visited. Now she needed to visit the seaside city, the home of her mother's birthplace as well as an aunt she never knew about. Oh, and a cat also. Thank you, Auntie!

ABOUT THE AUTHOR

Gary J. Rose was born in Hayward, California. There he attended public schools culminating in his graduation from the University of San Francisco. He rose to the rank of sergeant with the Milpitas Police Department and later was forced to retire due to a disability. During his employment with the police department, he was trained as a police hostage negotiator by the FBI. Following his retirement, he spent years as a private police background investigator. He then spent five years working for Philips Semiconductors in Sunnyvale, working corporate security.

Bored with retirement, he obtained two teaching credentials and, due to his law enforcement background, began a long teaching career with the Placer County Office of Education, where he was assigned to the county's juvenile detention facility.

Late in his career as an educator of at-risk juveniles, he was asked to create a military-style bootcamp academy for juvenile delinquents. From those three years as lead teacher of the academy, his cadets published their experiences in the novel, Hitting Rock Bottom which landed on Amazon's best sellers list for 10-weeks. He continued his education eventually earning his Doctorate in Social Psychology.

He later returned to the classroom teaching at the college/university level, and then five years working with adult inmates in Placer County jails. He finally retired in September 2021 so he could spend more time writing – his new passion. To date, he has written seven Jeannie Loomis thriller/adventure novels, his latest being The Fourth Reich.

Currently living in the foothills of northern California, he will be relocating to Myrtle Beach, South Carolina where he hopes to "live the dream."

www.ingramcontent.com/pod-product-compliance
Lightning Source LLC
Chambersburg PA
CBHW060549310726
48982CB00008B/1068/J

* 9 7 8 1 7 3 4 8 5 2 4 7 9 *